Kings of Aselvia

MOONSCRIPT
COLLUSION

Crowns of Aselvia
CROWN OF SAND & SEA

Other Works
FAIREST SON

CROWN OF SAND & SEA

H. S. J. WILLIAMS

H. S. J. WILLIAMS

To the Deliverer of bright futures and new dreams

The North

N

Here once stood
TERTOREM

OOLUM

Ocean

Brivan

This is a companion novella to MOONSCRIPT. Reading

MOONSCRIPT first is highly encouraged.

PROLOGUE

Wind and wave blew to and fro and who could say what guided them? The same could be said of Captain Coren of the *Solitary Star*.

Ask exactly who he was and different folk would give different answers. To most of the city of Oolum, he was simply the independent owner of a respectable merchant ship. To a few he was known as a smuggler, even a pirate—not of illegal wares, but of freedom—spiriting away slaves to a new life. Because of this, he was a hated legend to traffickers, somehow always slipping through their nets. To his wife he was a savior, friend, and partner, both in dance and in so-called crime. To his newborn son he was a star in the heavens.

To the elves, far off in Aselvia, he was a prince.

One wouldn't guess that bit by looking at him. There was a beard, for one. A small patch of red under his lip, and everyone knew elves didn't grow beards. (It was, in fact, glued on.) His shock of short and wild red hair hid his pointy ears or was otherwise bound by a brightly-hued bandana and sometimes a tri-corn hat. His skin was ruddy from the constant sun, even slightly weathered by the harshness of salt.

If there was one indication of his true nature, it was the fact that he wasn't aging. He'd only lived in Oolum for the past nine years or so, and thus far he could still give the appearance of a young man who was keeping his youth well into his thirties.

At some point, he knew that would have to change. It was either leave—and he wasn't doing that—or add aging into his disguise and act the part. Which wasn't that much of a stretch; he was already an expert at disguise. People mistakenly assumed the patch he wore meant he was missing an eye, when in fact he could see fairly well through the thin black cloth.

Oh yes, and there was one more thing Coren was known as—this a generally accepted fact by most—he was a good man.

As an independent merchant captain, he ought to have been rich, and there were some who whispered he had a stash hidden on some secret island, but most people knew good and well that Coren spent any extra money he had on helping anyone in need.

But no matter who Coren was known as, there were few who actually knew him well. Few who knew his story.

So perhaps, in the end, Captain Coren was simply this—

A mystery.

1

OOLUM

The *Solitary Star* had just docked in the Oolum port. Amid the flock of white-sailed galleons, its red sails burned like embers in the late afternoon sun, the daring cut of them sharp against the blue sky. A Brivanni corsair, most guessed, though it seemed a unique build.

Coren took his post at the gangplank as his sailors unloaded the cargo. This time, he had not headed the voyage, but he trusted his first mate to have done the job well, and they had returned with the supplies he'd ordered. Supplies that were now being loaded into carts, ready to be distributed around the city to those who needed them.

He double-checked each crate as it came down, marking them off on his list, then started helping the men load the final boxes into the waiting wagons.

One of the last crates held a long wooden box filled with layers of dried leaves. The box was simple, as he'd requested, to avoid attention, but he knew the gentle aroma the moment he peeked beneath the lid. Ilolieth, an herb grown in Aselvia that supported recovery of a weakened body. The king had sent it to Dormandy, just as he'd promised.

He was too busy smiling to himself to notice the tall, slim figure coming down the gangplank behind the sailors.

"Excuse me," a polished male voice said.

Coren flung a glance over his shoulder, taking in vague details— young man, fair, thin, middle class suit of Dormandy style, glasses, grey cap. In other words, someone who could wait.

"One moment," he hollered, turning back to what he was lifting. He heaved, setting the final few crates into the cart, and then pressed a few coins into the hand of the delivery boy.

"What's your business?" he asked the stranger, wiping an arm across his eye without turning around.

"Coren, it's me," the man said, voice thinly accented, barely able to be heard over the rattling of the retreating wagon.

4

Every muscle in Coren's body jerked. He spun and stared at the man in full this time, and yes—

Yes, it was him.

The steward of Aselvia, lord among elves.

His father, Leoren.

"Brights," he swore, stumbling backwards, then forward. Questions leapt to his tongue as a thousand scenarios whirled through his mind, every one of them an emergency. But there was no good asking here. If they made a scene of any kind it would only mean that it would take longer before they could have a chance to speak in private.

"We can't talk here," he said instead. "Come on, I'll take you home." He shouted out his sudden departure to his second mate, then grabbed his father's arm and headed into the crowd.

Usually the chaotic streets of Oolum didn't bother him, but this was another matter. The last thing Coren needed was for some merchant to stop them, begging them to inspect jackets embroidered in saffron thread, or for some friend to recognize him and try to sweep by for a chat.

But at last, they did escape the merchant streets and headed for the living quarters, which were always quiet and dull as tombs this time of day. Nobody worried about guarding their possessions in their homes, indeed some houses had curtains instead of doors, for everyone in this part of the city would take their valuables with them, if they had anything that could be considered valuable.

Coren's home was likewise bare, with only a few bits of furniture. He kept dried food and clothes in the basement, and the trap door to that *was* locked, the key on a long leather string about his neck.

"Sparks upon us, you gave me a start," Coren exclaimed, shutting the door behind them the moment they entered.

The little sandstone room glowed bright from the sun sweeping in through the narrow windows and bouncing off the walls.

He was out of breath and not from the fast pace at which he'd dragged both of them here. No, it had taken a great deal of effort to calmly escort his father to a private place they could talk without acting as if something was amiss. And something definitely had to be amiss. It was not like Leoren to just come visit. He never had before. Granted, he generally had no idea where to even find his son, so Coren couldn't really hold that against him.

He flung himself onto the nearest chair and reached up to push the eye patch off his face, rubbing at the perfectly fine eye underneath. "You wouldn't think that little bit of material could make one sweaty, but it sure as fire does. Not something I considered when I made it part of my daily accessories."

When Leoren didn't respond, he folded his arms across his chest. "Well, what's happened? Is it Errance? Are the borders safe?"

Instead of answering at once, his father took off the cap, revealing his long hair tied up in a neat bun at the nape of his neck. He looked sweaty and uncomfortable in that suit and in this place. "Nothing is wrong. Rendar's power assures our borders will always be safe. And Errance is…just Errance."

"Did he come with you? Is he hiding on a ship somewhere?" That would make some sense, as Coren had invited his cousin to come and see the work being done in Oolum.

Leoren's brow wrinkled. "No, he's in Aselvia, where he should be."

And where I should be too, wouldn't you like to say, Coren thought a bit grimly. "How is he exactly?" It was hard to believe it had been over a year now since he'd found out his cousin lived at all. After such a long imprisonment, adjusting to normal life was a daunting challenge for him.

"Taking it day by day. It's a slow process, but reeducating himself has given him a new purpose."

Coren nodded, and an awkward silence stretched between them. There was another chair by the table, but Leoren hadn't taken it.

"What about him and Tryss? Anything happening there?"

Leoren stared. "What sort of thing?"

"Oh, come on, don't say you hadn't noticed!"

"Can't say that I have?"

Coren gave a chuckling groan. "Never mind then. What's this about? Are you here to speak with the merchant council?" As far as he knew, Leoren's travels as ambassador had kept him on the west side of the narrow gulf, but it could be that Errance was making his move as king and reaching out to further trade. Though it seemed a bit soon for such forward thinking.

Leoren only looked at him with the quiet, slightly hurt expression Coren was so used to seeing.

"Coren," he said softly. "I came to see you and my grandson. Is that so difficult to believe?"

A sharp pain stabbed through Coren's heart, and he wasn't sure if he kept a wince from showing on his face. It wasn't that he wanted to always think the worst of his father. It was just hard not to assume that his father wasn't thinking the worst of him, and it made him edgy. He knew he shouldn't still act that way. Things were much better than they'd used to be.

"Sorry," he murmured. "I just figured there was something political going on, there usually is. Zizain and Zoren are over at a friend's house, a young mother with her first child, and they won't be back till morning.

I just finished sending off a delivery to some of the folks in the eastern quarter, so I have some time to spend. We can go about the city if you like. Everyone is used to me chatting with someone or other. Say, which ship did you come in on?"

"Yours."

"Really? I didn't even notice you come down the plank. I'm surprised my first mate let you come, he's usually pretty tight about extra passengers without my approval, unless their dire straits are obvious."

"I think he recognized me," Leoren admitted. "From that time we sailed back with you from Tertorem. But he was good enough to play along with my disguise."

"As disguises go, I must say that I'm impressed. Those glasses are an excellent touch, it really sells the whole university student look."

"As it is…" Leoren touched the edge of the gold rims. "…I actually wear these now."

"What! Really?"

"Yes, Tellie noticed I squint looking at things far away, and when I admitted my vision was a little blurry, she insisted I try these. They are a rather recent design from Korince, and I really didn't want to—"

Coren gave a small laugh of delight. "I'm glad to hear she can make you take care of yourself! She must be magic!"

The mention of Tellie softened his father's face, as it always did. He'd always known his parents wanted another child, especially a girl, but he'd never imagined they'd adopt, least of all a human. It was wonderful and strange and perfect.

"I think she must be," Leoren said.

"So what will it be? A stroll about town? We were rushing through it, so I don't imagine you saw much."

"Actually…I was hoping there could be a chance for us to talk." He reached for the empty chair, pulling it back from the table and easing himself onto it with the quiet grace he always exuded.

"Talk?" That was probably the last thing Coren had expected to hear him say. They weren't good at talking. Unless it was arguing.

"Yes," his father continued. "Errance was asking me about your life story, and I filled in what I could, but…I don't know much after you left. We never really discussed it."

They'd never discussed it because his life decisions had always been a matter of significant stress to both his parents.

"Huh." Coren leaned back in his chair, throwing his legs up onto the table. Too late he remembered this was not the most dignified pose to strike in front of his father, but well, they had agreed to disagree long ago. "Where do you want me to start?"

"The beginning, if you please." Leoren said. "Even back into your childhood. I always saw things my way, perhaps it will help if you explain it from yours."

Childhood, eh?

Where all his troubles began.

2

ASELVIA

Past

He had been summoned to the king.

Coren knew his parents had not been pleased with the haircut, but this was far more serious than he'd supposed! To think he would be in more trouble for cutting his hair than for dunking that brat in the fountain the other day. Or maybe, he thought with a surge of his young heart, maybe this summons was for both.

The royal halls remained cool despite the summer heat and this, paired with the deafening silence, made the ten year old boy feel like he was walking to his doom. The only noise to be heard was the sound of his own footsteps, usually so soft and light, clumping against the tile.

He paused before the doors of the King's Hall and craned back his head to see their imposing height. Hesitant, he pressed against them, and they swung silently open under his small hands.

Of course he'd been in this hall many times. But always there had been life and laughter and crowds to hide in. Now it was empty. Empty and enormous, made more so by the tall throne at the other end where waited a lone and grand figure.

Swallowing down his sudden shyness, Coren straightened his shoulders and strode ahead. After all, it was just his uncle. Not the king of all Aselvia. Not the one and only Celestial in the Lower World. Just his uncle.

But Rendar Celestrum had never felt like much of an uncle to Coren. A good man with a kind smile for certain, but the boy had always thought him rather distant and sad. When people spoke to him, his eyes and smile would sparkle, but more often than not, Coren would notice that during feasts and meetings, his eyes would glaze over as if he were staring off into another world and his smile would fade to something far more sorrowful and lonely.

Coren was only ten, but he had sharp ears, sharp eyes, and an even sharper mind. He'd heard that the king had not always been this way, no, that he had changed when he'd lost his son.

Coren's cousin. It was dreadfully unfair that his only cousin died years before he'd had the chance to meet him. In his mind, his cousin would have been his age and partner in crime, despite the paintings of the elegant adult prince to contradict him.

One of those paintings looked down on him now with an absolutely disapproving gaze. Coren's courage shrank a little as he drew closer to the throne and the king that waited.

At last, his faltering steps ceased altogether still some distance from the bottom of the stairs, and he waited, twisting his fingers together nervously. He couldn't look up at the king. No, the king was too bright, too beautiful, too perfect. Everything that made him squirm, but embodied in this great man, it made him tremble.

A soft swish of cloth against marble jerked his attention up, and he saw that the king had risen from the throne and now descended the stairs. Coren remained frozen, not caring how impolite it was to make the royal ruler walk all the way to him. His gaze darted here and there like a hunted rabbit desperate for escape.

A strong, gentle hand came to rest on his head. He flinched, feeling the long fingers examine the short strands of hair. When no rebuke or response of any kind came, the boy looked up again. Looked up, up, up into the face of the king.

"Does it stay out of your way now?" Rendar asked with a smile.

Coren's mouth dropped open and his eyes grew round in shock. "Yes!" he gasped. To think the great and glorious king would have guessed the reason for his deplorable action.

"It is a hassle," Rendar said, reaching back to touch his own smooth and silken hair. "Sometimes I believe it is only part of our culture to teach us patience." His eyes softened and he ruffled Coren's spikey scalp. "But there are other ways for you to learn that virtue, hmm?"

"Yes!" the boy said again, hardly believing his good fortune. Then, too proud to allow a false hope, added, "You aren't upset?"

"It's just hair," Rendar said with a shrug, taking his hand and leading the way to the foot of the steps where they both sat. "However," he began, and the boy drooped. "However, I have heard other things not pleasing. You make a nuisance of yourself to your elders and peers. As king, I look to the peace of my people, even down to the smallest child, and your mischief has not gone unnoticed. Some acts are harmless, yes, but others are filled with spite not befitting anyone, least of all a prince."

There it was. Prince. Oh, how Coren had come to hate that word. It seemed to be the final stamp of his parents' speeches, as if by reminding him of his station, he would repent and mend his ways. Prince, the boy surmised, meant perfection. Prince meant being like that man painted in the hall, who looked altogether unlike his dream playmate.

He stiffened, his chin jutting out and his brows knitting into a fierce knot. He watched that thoughtful expression appear on his uncle's face, the one that adults wore when they wondered, sometimes aloud, why Ayeshune had seen it fit to give such a fiery child to the gentle Casara and poor Leoren.

"A prince," Rendar continued, "is not about appearance or wealth or power. The people are not for the prince. A prince is to be a servant to his people. Our role as rulers is to serve, not to be served. And as such, you must practice kindness and respect."

"He was all but *asking* to be pushed into the fountain!" Coren burst out.

A smirk twitched across Rendar's lips, but he replaced it with a stern, raised eyebrow. "And the library?"

"Just a joke," he mumbled, hunching his shoulders.

"I know. But the keepers spent several hours making sure everything was back in place, and that stress was not needed. Also, suppose I had needed an important book that very second, and it couldn't have been found?"

"Oh!" Coren cringed. "That didn't actually happen...did it?"

"No," Rendar said. "Not this time. But you're old enough to start considering the consequences of your actions."

A knot formed in Coren's throat, and he huddled deeper into himself. For the first time in a long while, he felt sincerely guilty and upset for displeasing. "I'm sorry," he whispered. "I really am sorry about that. And I'll try to do better. But—" He held a hand to his hair and turned a pleading face to his uncle. "But Daava and Maava also get upset at me for things like this and for wanting to go explore Orim and things like that. I'm just curious, that's all."

Rendar leaned forward, crossing his arms over his upraised knee. A strange expression had come across his face, very like the sad and lonely one Coren was so used to seeing. This time it was stained with regret. "What are you curious about?" the king asked softly.

"Oh, just the other races, you know? And why we stay in Aselvia all the time? Daava is the ambassador and goes out so often, but he always avoids my questions, and says it's best to stay here. But why?"

After a long and dreadful silence, Rendar stirred and rose. "Come," he said. "There's someone I'd like you to know about. Someone I wish you could have met."

"Errance?" he said, thinking of all the times his mother had hinted that something terrible had happened to the dead prince for going outside of the protected borders.

"Of course I wish you could have met him," Rendar said sadly. "But I was speaking of someone else. Your other uncle."

"I have another uncle?" Coren cried.

"Cerand. Your mother's elder brother who was like a brother to me. And he would have been a far better teacher to you than I. But he…left us long ago."

Another someone he would never know. If the King had lost his wife, son, and someone like a brother, Coren began to understand why his gaze held so much sorrow.

Rendar was almost to the wall behind the throne and he paused there, waiting for the boy to catch up. Coren leapt to his feet and hurried over, heart pounding with curiosity. He'd explored many rooms of the castle, but he'd never gone here to the king's council chamber where he could retreat for privacy or discussion. The door was covered by a tapestry, probably for decoration rather than concealment. The door had that slight shimmer surrounding it that said this was one of the places Rendar had cast his shield magic, if magic it could be called. The light, barely visible, followed his command once cast, and allowed only those he willed to pass through. The wall that surrounded Aselvia only permitted elves and whoever they led inside. Other walls, like the one high up in the king's tower, were more particular. In that chamber, the Moonscript was kept, and only the king and those with the king's light could enter. This room, on the other hand, was probably something only for the king and his guests.

Coren skittered inside and stared hungrily at all the new things as the door closed behind him. At first glance, there didn't seem to be anything interesting. It was that sort of boring room where adults liked to relax, read books, and write letters. There were more paintings on the wall, and the largest painting, which hung above the desk, was a portrait of the king and queen.

There were many such portraits throughout the castle. This one stood out from the rest because there was a third member in the party. In the painting, someone perched on the wall just behind Rendar and Cerene. He was small, almost childlike, though a certain deadly strength corded his body. His face was young, even for elfkind. Those dark eyes so large in such a small, impish face. Black hair swept over his brow and to his shoulders. Delicate lines of thorns and flowers scrolled across his cheek and brow. It was a strange thing to include in a portrait painting,

because Coren had never seen elves draw on themselves for any lasting effect.

"The Dark Days left many with scars," Rendar said. "Cerand carried more than most. He never found peace here. He wasn't sure he'd find it anywhere. But he asked to serve me outside the borders of Aselvia. For years, he was my spy. Later...he served as the guardian for the remaining daishas."

Oh. Coren knew that story. The daishas, save one, had all been massacred by the chemas long before he'd been born. If his uncle Cerand had been guarding them when that happened...that explained his absence.

So another cautionary tale on why leaving Aselvia would only end in doom.

He sighed.

"He isn't dead, Coren," Rendar said.

Like a puppet on a string, Coren's head jerked up, eyes rounding in astonishment. "Then—what? Where is he?"

"As I said, he could not seem to find peace here. After the attack on the daishas, he cut ties with Aselvia and left no trace for me to follow. I only hope whatever path he chose will eventually lead him back here. Back home."

Coren sighed again. Dead or alive, it still seemed like a cautionary tale.

"I do not tell you this to make you sad or scared," Rendar said, noticing his glum expression. "Cerand fully knew the dangers of the world, but he went out anyway. That was his choice, and I respected it. The reason we stay here is on account of what we suffered in the past. But it is not forbidden to leave, not when you are of age, it is simply considered wise to remain in Aselvia considering the troubles we've had with other races. Relations with humankind are better now, but the scars of enslavement do not fade well, and as for the chemas, we have continuous conflict. The aliths…" He paused, a fond look coming across his features. "…have a good history with us, but they are rather far north. However, when you are a man, you may seek your own destiny as Cerand did. But for now you are a young son, and you must honor your parents. Please try to respect their wishes."

After a pause, Coren gave a small bow. It made sense. It was the right thing to do. It couldn't be that hard.

For the record, he really did try.

He exchanged mischief for merriment (mostly), he threw himself into his studies (often), he made friends instead of enemies (for the most part), and he kept his hair long as befitting his culture (begrudgingly).

But as year by year went by, the more Coren wondered if he'd really been cut out to be an elf. Being a prince was most definitely a mistake. It wasn't that life was miserable. On the contrary, life in Aselvia was unquestionably fine. Yet…something was missing. And he couldn't help but wonder if that missing something was out *there*. Perhaps it was what had called the princes before him. But every time he brought up the subject of leaving, which he often did, his father would get that terrified, troubled look in his eyes and shut the idea down. Of course, they probably thought he would not only be the third prince to leave, but also the third prince to never return. For that, he couldn't blame them.

Still, it wasn't fair, not when his father was ambassador, passing beyond the border at least once per year and Coren had never been allowed to go with him. He'd even suggested that he train under his father to be ambassador; the idea had actually excited him. He was sure he could be good at it, people told him he'd become charming as a young man. But that suggestion too had been waived.

So resentment sank its little fangs into his heart, and he began to pick up rebellion once again—and this time intentionally. Small things.

For the most part. He didn't actually want to be a trouble to the kingdom. But just enough that his parents noticed. He'd tried it their way. They still treated him like he would shatter if he stepped on something wrong.

And then he did.

It happened by chance, really.

Just one night, as he'd returned from after-dark adventuring and had decided to enter his room via the stout vines crawling up the wall to his window. It wasn't as if he actually had a reason to sneak about, he was just in that sort of mood. And when his mood turned suddenly to wanting food, he followed that urge too.

But just at the top of the stairs, he heard his parents' raised voices from the parlor below. He paused, knowing he shouldn't eavesdrop, but the conversation had *that* sort of tone, the heavy worrisome one that his parents used when discussing his latest rebellions.

Don't listen. It will just be the same thing, the same disappointment. You don't need to hear any of that.

But he crouched with cat-like grace and listened anyway.

"I just know the moment he is of age, he is going to be across the border in a shot," Leoren was muttering. "And we might never see him again."

"You should take him with you on one of your ambassador journeys," Casara suggested. "Let the excitement wear down while he is still able to be guided by us."

"But Errance—"

"He isn't Errance. I don't think there is anyone out there who is seeking to destroy him."

"But what if when he sees the outside world, he is still enamored with it?"

She was quiet.

Coren had just about decided to move on—it wasn't as if he hadn't heard similar conversations before—when his father spoke again.

"It's my fault."

Casara inhaled sharply. "Leo, no."

"It could be, couldn't it? Your brother certainly thought I was unworthy of you. My tainted blood come back to haunt me."

"As if blood has anything to do with it. You were never affected by any so-called haunting."

"Possibly only because of my complete determination to reject it. I don't know. Maybe not telling Coren was a mistake."

"Telling him? He's a child!"

"He isn't anymore. And the longer we wait, the harder it will be for him to accept."

"I don't see why it needs to be brought up at all! There is no point in it. It is something in the past. It's not haunting us now; it has nothing to do with you or us!"

Coren's heart was beginning to hammer in his ears with enough thunder to drown the argument out. What was this about?

But the conversation did not continue for Casara stormed from the room, too upset to speak further. After a few moments, some of the lights flickered out, blown away by a puff of breath, then a single glow came gliding down the hall towards the stair. Coren knew he should move before he was seen, but he couldn't. So he sat still and waited.

The glow preceded a candle held by his father. Leoren had already started up the stairs, eyes on each step and brow furrowed with thought, when he noticed his son sitting just above him. He drew back as if seeing a ghost.

"Coren! What...how long have you been here?"

Coren stared at him, gut twisting. "What were you talking about?"

"What do you mean?"

"You know what I mean. That haunting thing you were discussing."

"Coren, it's late, I really don't think that now—"

He was *not* letting that excuse stop him. "Tell me."

Rubbing a hand down his face, Leoren looked past him into the shadows of the room. Bleak darkness reflected in his eyes, the lines of his face becoming strained. After several tense moments, he finally spoke. "I am half-elf. Half...human."

Coren blinked. Both his grandparents on his father's side were elves, decidedly so.

"Your grandfather, Torlief, is not my father. I was born in the Dark Days, a result of one of our captor's cruelties. The chances for children of such an act were slim to nothing, yet still...I was born, and my mother chose to love me as her own. She could barely take care of herself as it was, so that was when Torlief stepped in and offered his hand in marriage so that both she and I could be looked after. He became my father when I was young but still old enough to have realized the truth. It has haunted me all my life. The idea that I should not exist."

Coren had been holding his breath, and now it broke from him with the sharpness of glass. "How...how is that your fault?"

"Everyone told me it wasn't," Leoren said with a weak shrug. "Maava told me so, Daava told me so, as did Rendar and Cerene and your mother. But I still felt like I had something to prove. That I wasn't going to be anything but an elf and my mother's son, and so I threw myself into being useful and…worthy. I'm sure you've heard the stories of how long it took me to propose to your mother. I sometimes wonder if I would have held my tongue forever, but after the loss of Cerene and then Errance, it seemed to me that life was fleeting. If there was any way I could bring brightness to Casara's heart, then I could not keep my love for her silent."

It was beginning to make a sort of sick sense, all of his father's insecurities, all the doubts, all the—but even at the same moment that Coren felt pity, a red anger blossomed in a stain across his heart.

"So you think I'm a mistake too," he said, voice coming out as harshly as he intended.

His daava stared at him, turning pale. "What…? No…no, I never said that."

"You did! You said 'tainted blood coming back to haunt you.' Am I that haunting? Are you telling me you think I am who I am because of some sick monster a thousand years ago?!"

"No—"

"You DO!" His vision was beginning to blur, and his throat closed after that final shout. He could barely see his father flinch and he barely cared. Without waiting for another objection, he turned on his heel and ran.

A lattice of light and shadow always hung in the palace temple, cast from both the trees and woven ceiling. In truth, the temple looked more like a wild grove than a building, with the mossy pillars seeming to have grown right up alongside the trees and wildflowers. A white stone fountain bubbled in the midst of it, overgrown with vines and lichen. The holy writings were not kept in this place, and the priest did not live under its roof (though he could often be found there), so Coren had once wondered why it was called a temple at all. It was perhaps best described as a place of refuge, a promised harbor for peace, prayer, and counsel.

He'd come often throughout his childhood, first in curiosity, and then in honest seeking. He liked the priest, Oriah, a man who never seemed to hold his exploits against him. For an elf, Oriah was rather plain, but what one really noticed was the constant sparkle in his deep brown eyes and the way a smile always tugged at the corners of his mouth, as if he and God were having some amusing conversation.

"What latest atrocity have you committed now?" The priest rose from the garden with a trowel in hand as Coren walked in through the archway, that warm smile as familiar as the sun spreading across his face.

"Existing, apparently."

The smile faltered, just for a moment, before Oriah nodded sagely. "Ah. The eventual crisis of every man."

"Did you know about my father?" Coren went straight to the point, not in the mood for games. "About his bloodline?"

"Yes," Oriah said, not even blinking. "Everyone does. Well. Everyone alive during the Dark Days, that is."

"He only just told me."

"I suppose it is not an easy thing to tell one's son."

Coren sat on the edge of the fountain and plucked at the leaves of a small shrub, letting them drop one by one into the water, disturbing his reflection ripple by ripple. "Do you think it has any weight? Human blood, I mean. Do you think it made me this way?"

Oriah gave an indelicate snort. "Blood, eh? If a zealous spirit and a sense of adventure came from any side of the family, it would be your mother's."

"Uncle Cerand and Errance, you mean."

"Cerene too!"

"The *queen*?" It was hard to refer to her as his aunt, mainly because she'd died long before he was born, but also because everyone else called her the queen. It was hard to imagine such a description fitting the woman he saw in the paintings, always haloed by the celestial gift from her husband. She even had a *name* that sounded saintly.

"A firebrand, that one."

Coren shook his head in disbelief, but a soft grin stole onto his face. Imagine that.

Oriah reached over and ruffled his hair. "In all seriousness though, lad, your identity isn't defined by your family. It is given to you, a gift of the Lord's, and the choices with it. Perhaps this desire for the outside world isn't a thing of evil, but a calling from Ayeshune himself."

"That's a nice thought."

"You doubt? You consider it a selfish, frivolous desire?"

Coren hesitated. "I know that's what everyone seems to think...that I'm just restless and unsatisfied with life here...that I'll chase forbidden things once I'm out...but...that's not it. Not really. I just want to know what else is out there. It was all made by God, wasn't it? I want to see it. I want to know what the other races are like. I want..."

"Knowledge. Experience. Empathy." Oriah tapped the small trowel in his hand against the stone with each word, every beat ringing. "Powerful tools that can be used for great things."

"Could you tell Daava that?" Coren said, burying a chuckle into his fist. "It sounds so noble when you say it."

"He will see it," Oriah answered. "If you take such a path, then one day he will see it."

3

OOLUM

Present

O utside, the sun was beginning to set, and darkness swallowed the small room. Coren struck a match and held it to a candle, the wick catching with a hiss. Long shadows swept out to dance upon the surrounding walls. Pulling a pitcher from the cupboard, he poured a golden drink into two mugs.

"That's not liquor, is it?" Leoren asked.

"Saints, Da, you think I would give you liquor? I don't drink the stuff anyway, unless it's part of some deception. As a matter of fact, it is turmeric tea, sweetened with honey, imported, and rather rare. Has medicinal benefit, the healers would love it. Especially Mister Calming Teas, can't remember his name now, it started with an Ah."

"Ahspen?"

"Yeah, that one."

Leoren took a curious sip, and his brows rose in appreciation. "I will definitely need to add this to the list of imported goods we trade for." After another sip, he said in a soft voice, "I never knew you and Oriah were close."

"He had a sense of humor and listened to me. I liked it when people listened. Grandmother was good at it too, though of course she never had much to say."

"I talked too much, didn't I? Scolded and reformed."

"I mean, you said it, not me."

Leoren's mouth twitched. "I never forgave myself for casting my own anxiety and fruitless self-loathing onto you. You must know I deeply regretted it."

"Never mind. I didn't let it cling to how I saw myself. And I figured you were trying to make up for it when you brought me to Dormandy on your ambassador journey that very same year. And every year following."

With a sigh, Leoren leaned forward, arms on his knees. "When you came of age and went off on your own, you never did tell me exactly how it went. The details, I mean."

"Details?" Coren chuckled. "Well. It rained."

4

DORMANDY

Past

Rain in Dormandy was nothing like rain in Aselvia.

In the land of elves, everything was green—the forests, the hills, the valleys. Even when the rain fell so thickly that the horizon was swallowed up, it held the mysterious color of lavender mist. A rich aroma of wet earth and grass rose into the air and opened the lungs with every cleansing breath.

In Dormandy, everything was grey. And despite the fact that most of the buildings and streets were made of stone, there seemed to be mud everywhere. Not a healthy brown mud, but a dark grey, gloopy, and very sticky sort of mud.

Even so, no amount of water could wash away Coren's smile as he strode through the city. He had not traveled by foot all this way, instead releasing his horse to return home some distance off the main road. From here, he intended to travel by ship for a while. He might have had the mind to explore the city some, but after a few visits in his youth with his father, his horizons were already reaching farther. He'd glimpsed that great grey sea just once, and it had sparked a fire within him. They said the vast water was but a long gulf into Orim, splitting it into the West and East, but that further south it opened into a vast ocean that hid hundreds, maybe thousands of islands.

He'd heard ships were funded by the Dormandy University to explore those islands and bring back strange and new things, and that the sea captains would hire anyone crazy enough to do it.

Crazy, eh? That suited him.

He'd never walked the common streets of this city till now. The buildings hunkered much closer together, the streets were narrower and worn so that enormous puddles of water pocketed the stones. Each house was at least three stories tall, sometimes even six, all the windows facing the road. And everywhere, absolutely everywhere, people scurried about their daily duties, even on such a wet day.

Coren craned his head up to the brooding sky, watching the raindrops plummet past the roof peaks. That was why he noticed the window above him open and he watched as a pair of arms dumped a pot down towards the cobblestones. He had just enough good fortune to leap out of the way in time.

For heaven's sake! Who in their right mind just flung dishwater out into a crowded street!

If it was dishwater.

Whatever it was, it was fast disappearing in the current of the gutter, but now he eyed the muddy eddies with more suspicion. A little bit of his enthusiasm dampened. Was it just the rainy days or were human cites always this dirty, and if so, how did anyone choose to live in such a way?

Alright, enough of this. Time to get out of the rain, find something hot to eat, and talk to some sailors. He'd heard enough about this city to know he could find all three at the chowder houses by the wharf.

The smell of salt and fish grew ever stronger the further he went, and the road itself began to slant downwards, the gutters running with a swift current of sludge. A crowd of folks clustered outside a ramshackle cottage stuck between two larger buildings. Coren took one look at the rain-stained sign hanging above the door. It was carved to resemble a fish standing on its upright fins, holding a bowl and spoon. Or at least he assumed that's what it was meant to depict.

He slipped past the leather-coated men just outside the door and ducked inside. The fish funk had a more welcoming aroma now, mixed with traces of cream and vegetables. Tables crowded inside the small room, every single one of them occupied, but a few stools were empty along the wooden counter next to the kitchen. He squeezed in between two brawny sailors and waited for the maid behind the bar to take notice and ask for his order.

The man next to him noticed first and leaned in. "Hey there, sweetheart, what are you doing in this part of town?" The other sailor opposite him guffawed.

Sweetheart. Really?

He'd had enough sense not to stroll into town looking completely like an elf. He knew humans had opinions on elvish beauty and the last thing he wanted was to stand out or be underestimated. His clothing was simple and he'd tied his hair back—yes, he had not cut it yet, because that seemed too much like adding insult to the injury of his parents' hearts, and he knew long hair still held fashion for some men in Orim.

Did he really look that much different?

"Funny," he muttered.

"Nah, don't look away, where did you come from? Some fancy Korince brat?" The sailor made a grab for his chin, and Coren only just swerved back in time.

"Hands off," he snapped.

The laughter flickered out of the sailor's eyes, and both he and his comrade grew ugly sneers. "You have a lot of nerve, coming in here as if you own the place."

Own...what were they talking about? Couldn't they just take a hint and leave him alone?

He moved to stand, but one of them grabbed his arm.

"He said 'hands off,' didn't he?" A shadow cast over the three of them, a mountain of a man blocking out the light of the hung lanterns. The baritone of his voice rattled the floorboards beneath their feet.

The sailors didn't even take a moment to consider their chances. They simply dropped Coren's arm and slunk away.

Coren squinted at his unexpected ally, trying to discern some features in the silhouette, but the man turned and beckoned. "Sit with me, lad. I assume you're here looking for a crew to join. Friendly advice— don't choose that one."

"I like that advice." Coren followed him to a booth tucked in the corner and sat across from him. His breath caught. He'd never met a man like this one.

First, he had to be the size of the legendary General Reyin. Second, his skin was as dark and shining as ebony, reflecting the flames that flickered in the white bone lamps. His hair was thick, corded, and glittering with silver.

"My name is Captain Ulio. I'm looking to hire a few more hands for a voyage to the southwest islands, a commission by Dormandy University. It will be a few months at sea at the least, not exactly easy for a first-timer. You'd be better sailing a few merchant runs across the gulf. But I'll bring you on if you think you have what it takes."

Coren barely absorbed anything he said, but the final few words took hold. He certainly did not feel like he had what it took, not in comparison to this magnificent captain who looked as if he wrestled the ocean for fun. Where was he from—Oolum, Brivan maybe?

"Well, lad? Haven't got all day."

"Yes!" he blurted. Some part of his mind that far too closely resembled his father made a shrieking sound, and he stuffed it down. He'd come for this kind of job, and this man seemed noble enough.

"Good." The table creaked as the man rose to his feet. "You may find it easier to climb the rigging if you cut your hair, but one thing...keep it shaggy about the ears."

OOLUM

Present

"He already knew what you were?" Leoren's mouth parted in surprise.

"Yeah, I guess I wasn't so good at disguises back then. But Ulio also had a keen eye that looked for secrets about a man. He always said he needed to be discerning when choosing crewmates, because the last thing you wanted was to be stuck out at sea with a person you couldn't trust."

5

THE SOUTHERN SEA

Past

I grew up surrounded by beauty, but now I've discovered true paradise on this earth. The southern islands are the closest thing to heaven I could have imagined. Azure waters encircle the land, crystal clear windows to a landscape of bright colors and living jewels. When I dive into the waves, rejuvenating warmth washes across my skin. There is colorful seagrass, but also a strange hard rock the sailors call coral that is sharp to the touch. There are little plants that move with a life and intelligence of their own, and the fish here glitter with every hue of the rainbow. Giant sea turtles gently float through the current, sometimes bumping into my shoulder. Their eyes are kind and soulful. I *pry up clams from the rocks and crack them open on the sandy shore. Sometimes I'm lucky enough to find a pearl. The trees are strange, long trunks bending upwards, crowned with a sharp-bladed bush. The fruit can be drilled in order to drink its inner milk or cracked open to reveal its flaky flesh.*

Coren paused and leaned back in his hammock, the ink at the end of the quill scratching a beard on the end of his chin. Who was he writing this for anyway? A letter back home? No, that would likely send his parents into a panic that he was never coming back. For himself? Why not! He didn't trust his memory to keep all the details. And he never wanted to forget a thing.

The creak of a floorboard caught his ear, even above the perpetual groan of the ship's hull, and he looked up to see the first mate peering at him through the door. "The cap'n wants you above board."

Surprised, Coren capped his bottle of ink and tucked it under a thin blanket with his quill and journal. Not that it would stop any snooping sailor, but it wasn't an open invitation.

A chill wind kissed his cheek as he reached the top of the stair. A canvas of dark sky, hung with stars, spread out above. No storms, no rough water, just a perfect clear night for swift sailing. But something was wrong. The lanterns. Usually their golden glow spread across the ship, but not a single one was lit. He squinted in what little light could be gathered by the stars, and found the massive silhouette of the captain up on the quarterdeck.

The man did not look his way as he came up alongside him, only continued staring off across the waters. He lifted a finger and pointed. "See that, lad?"

Coren squinted, eyes still adjusting to the dark. "Another ship? They have only a few lanterns, hard to see."

The captain handed him his spyglass. "Take a look at the flag."

Raising the glass to his eye, Coren looked first at the masts and then across the rest of the ship. "I don't see one."

"Aye. No flag, low lights. Sure signs of someone who doesn't want to be caught."

"Pirates?"

"Worse, slavers."

Coren blinked, handing the spyglass back. "It's not allowed in West Orim."

"Aye, but the East runs on the back of slaves. It's an easy thing for a person to be taken from Dormandy or Korince, shipped across to Brivan or the like, and never heard from again. But taking natives from the islands is even easier. Many do not speak the common tongue, and they have no way of finding their way back. Don't think it's just the East cities that take them either. Korince may have laws against slavery, but they don't do much to stop it. Many things are done in the dark."

A cold shudder crawled across Coren's skin, never mind the warmth in the air. "Silver saints…is there anything we can do?"

The captain cleared his throat, a deep thrumming sound within his chest. He withdrew a medallion from a fold of his tunic and held it out for Coren to see. The details were a bit hard to make out in the dark, but it appeared to depict a hawk biting the neck of a snake. "I did not tell you this from the start, but I am also licensed by the Dormandy government to apprehend any slave ships found in their waters."

"We aren't anywhere near Dormandy waters."

The captain's smile shone white. "Aye. But it's our word against theirs, isn't it? The crew is familiar with these ropes, but seeing as it's your first time, I thought it fit to give some explanation. The other ship may try to put up a fight, so are you handy with a sword?" He held one out as he spoke, wrapped in a leather scabbard.

"Yes, I've been trained."

"Have ya now. Ever killed?"

He hesitated as he reached for the blade. "Um. No."

"I would have hoped not, a fresh lad like you. Hopefully it won't come to that, but just in case." He clapped the sword into Coren's palm. "All the same, you keep in the crow's nest till this is over."

"But I'd like to help!"

"Best help is to observe how it's done and keep an eye out for any tricks they may try to pull." With that said, Captain Ulio turned and began calling orders to his crew in his hushed, deep tones that almost blended in with the ocean waves.

Knowing by now that argument with the captain was pointless, Coren headed up the rigging for the crow's nest. Once at the top, he knelt behind the wooden bars, not wishing to stick out as an obvious target once the fighting began.

He could hear the wood groaning and gears turning as the ballista were uncovered and primed for fire. Their giant grappling hooks were attached to thick ropes that coiled on spools. When Coren had discovered them under the canvas a few days ago, he'd asked about their purpose. "Fishing," he'd been told.

Fishing indeed.

The Crimson Crane cut through the waters, creeping up on the other ship like a snake pursuing its prey. Its red sails and dark wood would not be easily seen in the dark, and they drew so near the opposing vessel that the laughter of the other sailors could be heard over the rolls of the waves.

The captain could not be seen by every man on deck, but still there was an aura of waiting for a signal. What that signal would look like, Coren did not know, but he figured he'd know it when he saw it.

A flash. An arc of light. And then a burst of fire in the air.

Yes, that was some signal, alright.

The ballista cracked, the hooks shooting across the gap to grip the wooden rails of the ship. The ship moaned, the ropes creaked, and voices shouted from both sides as Ulio's crew began cranking the wheels to pull the vessels together. As the sides collided with a thundering swell, sailors began throwing over ladders and securing ropes. The crew was across, Ulio at their head, but just enough time had passed for the slavers to gather their wits to meet them in battle.

The clash of steel rattled even to the marrow of Coren's bones and the shouts and cries of the struggle would echo in his ears for weeks afterward.

From his loft, he couldn't see much detail of what was happening on the other ship, but he felt the moment the winds changed. That sudden inhale when a gust catches under the sails. An aching groan rippled from the belly of the ship as both vessels began to pull away from each other, caught only by the ropes tying them together. The hulls spread apart, tipping the masts together.

Coren clung to his cage as wood, rope, and canvas tangled together. The screams of the sailors rang out beneath him, and he didn't need to look to know that both crews were hauling at the ropes, trying to pull the ships back together, lest they drag each other into the sea.

Then he was moving. Most of him didn't even know why. It was the sensible thing to remain tucked into his nest, but he had tasted the stinging salt on the wind, and he could not sit still. The wildness of the sea, its incomparable spirit, flowed through his blood and rushed into his lungs.

His captain was aboard the other ship. So he caught hold of the nearest rigging and began weaving his way across, dodging and ducking through the tangle of ropes and the buffeting blasts of wind and cloth.

Ulio fought just below him. He and the captain of the rival vessel crossed blades, but they were not the only ones on deck. Several members of the slaver crew were drawing near, swords at the ready, not about to let the fight conclude honorably.

Coren grabbed one of the loose ropes flopping about the sails, slashed his sword through the fibers, and swung down. His feet struck the nearest sailor first, toppling him over, but even then the momentum pushed him forward. At the very end of the swing, he launched, curling himself into a roll, and clattering across the wooden deck. He was back up on his feet, pulling his sword from its sheath, but one sailor was already charging at him. Really quite impressive, that sort of recovery. Coren ducked under the attack, punching him in the stomach with the hilt of his sword as he went past.

He could recognize other figures joining them, other members of his crew. Within a few short moments, they had overpowered their adversaries. The enemy captain's sword rattled on the wood as Ulio disarmed him and held him at sword's point.

As sailors began roping up the captors turned captives, Ulio turned and fixed Coren with a look. "Reckless boy," he barked. "I told you to stay in the crow's nest."

Coren's mouth twitched, unable to feel a bit of guilt. "You also told me to keep an eye out for any tricks they would pull. Which I was having a hard time doing from all the way over there."

Ulio smacked him alongside the head, but not hard enough to hurt. "Handy with a sword," he muttered. "I suppose I should have known you'd be a lot more handy than just that."

He turned back to the shackled captain, fixing him with a dour look. "This is a Dormandy galleon," he said. "And by the looks of it, you are of Dormandy blood."

"You have a lot of gall to assume that," the man spat.

"I will not have to assume once we search your cabin and find these ship's papers." As if on cue, Ulio's first mate came running up to his side, a stack of documents in his hand. Ulio took them and began flipping through. Whatever he was looking for, he quickly found it. The deadly gleam in his eyes sharpened as he looked up from under a hooded brow. "You are registered with Dormandy's merchant guild. For that, I will turn you in and they shall decide your fate." He flicked the papers back into the hand of his first mate and walked away, ignoring the string of profanities spewed after him.

Coren trotted after Ulio's heels, unsure of what to say or do.

"Ship searched and secure?" Ulio shouted.

"All clear, cap'n!" one of the men called back. "Still checking for any secret compartments, but the captives are down in the bilge."

A huge two-door hatch loomed in the aft deck of the ship. Ulio threw them open with a single heave, and they thudded against the wood with a damning drum. A wooden stair descended into the void, a vile stench rising to contaminate the pure night air.

Ulio, already a few steps down, paused in the dark mouth of the hatch and held out a hand. "Come 'ere, lad. I want you with me for this."

Every sailor near enough to hear paused what they were doing and looked Coren's way, a somber expression upon their faces. Coren felt his legs turn leaden, felt his heart sink into his gut. Swallowing, he pried his feet from the floorboards and forced himself to Ulio's side.

The darkness swallowed them up.

A sharp hiss and then light broke through the darkness. Ulio swept the flame from match to wick and then shut the case of his lantern. The match he bit in between his teeth, burnt end first.

The boards creaked and groaned with each step they took. But that was not the only sound. Murmurs of pain rippled through the shadows, sending a shiver through Coren's bones. At the bottom of the stairs, a sharper sound accompanied the moans, the clink of cold iron on iron.

The light cast upon the gleam of cage bars. They lined the hull of the ship. They did not hold a single person each, but were crammed with many bodies. Bodies that were chained even inside the bars. There were some whimpers of fear or growls of anger when the light cast into the shadows, but mostly there just came silence—a sick thickness like phlegm in the throat. A few eyes glittered in the brightness from the flame, a few teeth flashed.

"So many," Ulio murmured. "Enough for an entire village, although I suspect they took from multiple."

"You have the keys, yes?" Coren asked. It was taking all his strength not to gag at the stench of human waste soaked and baked into the wood. The sooner they could get everyone out of here the better.

"It is not that simple," Ulio said sadly, shaking his head. "They might attack us or jump overboard. First, I must attempt to establish some hope and trust." He cleared his throat and then spoke in rich, rolling words.

Coren had no clue what was being said, but he could feel the surprise and tremoring wonder stir through the slaves. And then—

"Ulio! Oi, Ulio! It is Kuah!"

"Kuah!" Ulio boomed, his tone blended in a strange mix of happiness and horror. He strode through the cages until he found the man pressed up against the bars, fingers eagerly reaching through. Setting the lantern upon the hook of the cage, Ulio set to work on the locks. "What are you doing here, Kuah?" he said as the door creaked open. "Is being captured once not good enough for you?"

"I try to stop them. Try to warn friends," Kuah said, the common language uncertain on his tongue, but his smile bright and universal as the sun. "But they take me again. And you here again." The chains fell from his hands, but rather than stepping at once from his prison, he turned to the huddled figures behind him, chattering excitedly in his own speech.

The rigid fear and confusion in the stale air slowly began to soften, and soon a few voices joined that of Kuah's in hopeful resonance. One by one, they stepped out of the cage, Ulio unlocking their chains, some massaging their limbs, some collapsing upon the floor weeping, others running to the other cages and calling out the good news.

Coren drew back against the wall, unable to breathe, unable to stop shaking. This sensation coursing through his body, what could he call it? It was almost like fear. He was certain it should be joy, but he was overwhelmed. It was one thing to hear of captivity in the history his family had briefly touched on, but it was another to see it. And that wild, chaotic, almost mad joy that gripped the air with a fierce energy seemed like something that could too easily spiral out of control.

But Ulio stood in their midst as an unwavering rock, and he gently took each one and freed them from their bonds. When all of them had been released, he raised his arms and spoke aloud in their language, till they hushed and bent forward to listen.

When he'd finished, he led the way up the stair, helping guide the weakest. A few glanced Coren's way in question, but most didn't even notice him.

A cheer arose from Ulio's sailors as they came up from the bilge onto the deck, quiet so as not to alarm, but warm enough to be welcoming. When Coren trailed after them a few moments later, he hurried to the side of the deck and watched from there. A quick look around told him that the original crew of this ship had been taken elsewhere. Wise. He couldn't imagine the anger or terror that would ensue if the former captives saw their captors.

The wind had steadied and there was a plank now drawn between the two ships. Ulio leapt onto a barrel and called out a few instructions, first in the unknown language, and then again in the common tongue. "We'll need our crew to split between ships. Most of you will take this ship back to Dormandy waters and turn it in. The rest shall return to *The Crimson Crane* and we will be taking these fine people home!"

The sailors cheered again, louder, and their new comrades joined the cheer with them.

6

THE ISLANDS

Past

The people of the islands were nearly as colorful as the flowers that festooned the foliage. All were deeply hued by the warmth of the sun, but their hair ranged from dark to pale to even red like Coren's own and their eyes glittered like jewels. Of all the races, humanity had been created with the widest range of appearance, chosen to spread out and inhabit the earth and progress with that swiftness in their nature. It seemed sad to him that so many humans spoke of the elves as if they were the most beautiful of all creatures, for he found their diversity more beautiful by far.

They had delivered the stolen people back to each of their islands, and more than once they had been attacked by a tribe fearing another ship had come to take more of their people away. But each time the fear and anger turned quickly to joy, although the ship did not stay anchored in one cove for long before moving on to the next island, until at last only Kuah and his people were left.

At Kuah's island, they laid anchor and took the small boat out to the island, others clambering into the canoes offered by the islanders who recognized the red sails and came out to meet them. They led them through the jungle to their village. Houses were built below and even upon the thick and wide-branched trees. The people danced and sang about the fires, inviting Ulio's crew to join them. The sizzling meat of pigs roasted above the fire-pits, and melons were broken in pieces and eaten straight off the rind.

"How did people even come to find these islands?" Coren had asked Ulio during the festivities.

The man gave him a sideways smile, seeming surprised to be asked such a question. "Does mankind need a reason to seek out the mystery of the far horizon? Do elves not have that yearning within them? You do, I think, at least. Still, though each tribe has their own story, all share a common theme. The first who voyaged out were fleeing some terrible enemy. Some say plague, some say monster, some say...a great darkness. A time in which the sun went out and the air turned cold."

"The Dark Days." Coren slowly nodded, imagining how many different people would have taken the risk of fleeing out to the unknown sea rather than stay on the mainland in that time of bloodshed and war. Little wonder then that the island people seemed to have the variety of all corners of humankind.

Now, having wandered from the village, well-fed and feet sore from dancing, Coren sat upon the shore. Waves lapped the rocks at his feet, foam catching on the craggy sides. Before him, the ocean glittered in silver and gold under the fading light of a sunset. The colors in the sky reminded him of a rose slowly opening, soft and pure at the center, turning peach to amber to darker hues of mulberry. Overhead, the sky was a deep blue, deep enough to be another ocean with clouds eddying across its surface in layers so complex that his eyes blurred when looking at them.

But even with such beautiful verse turned vision in front of his gaze, his thoughts kept returning to the dark hull of the ship, the smell of wretchedness kept gripping his throat. He rubbed at his temple as if he could blot the memory out. Why was he still thinking about that? They had saved the villagers, hadn't they? They'd returned them home, and

the warm taste of the meal prepared for them in thanks still settled in his stomach. So why would the nightmarish images not fade...?

A hand bumped his shoulder. Startled, he turned to see Ulio handing him a coconut broken in half. The man settled on the rock beside him, saying nothing as they both sipped the milk from their vessels.

"How old are you, lad?" Ulio asked.

"Twenty." The word came out a little choked, his throat thick with unshed tears.

"I figured you just looked young, but you really are, aren't you? What possessed you to come out here? Is it some rite of passage for elves that nobody knows about? Do you walk in secret among us all the time?"

"No. At least, no to the rite thing, and I don't know about the second. But as for leaving home...I dunno. I really don't. Guess I was looking for an adventure, which I certainly got. But maybe...maybe I was looking for a purpose."

"Sometimes purpose is something we give ourselves," Ulio said, crossing an arm over his knee. "You can't just sit on a shore and watch your prize bob out on the ocean, hoping the waves will guide it to you. You've got to swim for it. Grasp it. Never let it go."

"Is that how you started doing this?"

"I began as just a regular merchant, looking for new lands and new thrills, much like you. But when I saw that some ships were being hired to take the people of the islands as well as the goods, I knew I couldn't stand by and pretend it wasn't happening. So I chartered my ship under Dormandy's service. They're far from perfect themselves, but their sense of trade does believe in keeping good relations with the islanders as opposed to strife. With that reputation, I've established trade with some tribes farther out that would surround any other ship in their war canoes and burn it down with fire arrows. So I live my life, I have my adventure, and I can still sleep at night."

"Can you?" Coren rubbed at his eyes again. "I'm not sure I could."

The giant hand rested gently upon his shoulder. "You can't save them all, Coren," he said, voice deep and rumbling. "But it's better to save some than none at all. Once you accept that, you can find some measure of peace even as your drive increases."

"I just don't get it," Coren mumbled. "I don't get why people can be this cruel, this selfish. I don't see how Ayeshune allows it."

Ulio leaned back, contemplating both the sky and the comment. "Ayeshune, that's the name for the Old God, isn't it? I don't know very much about God, boy. But if there is one thing I have become more certain of in all my days, it is this—there cannot be such great wrong in the world unless we know that it is wrong, and there can be no standard for wrong unless there is an ultimate right. And that can only be such an unshakeable truth if it is the utmost power. So don't fret, lad. What is wrong will be made right, someday. In the meantime, we do what we can...we do what we can."

7

OOLUM

Present

The turmeric tea in Leoren's cup had long since gone cold. He'd just held it while listening, taking the occasional sip, but otherwise forgetting to finish it altogether. "What an incredible man," he said softly after a few moments had passed.

"Still the finest I've ever met," Coren agreed.

"Did he have anything personal driving him?"

"You mean a tragic backstory? No, no, nothing like that. He was just a native of Oolum who saw the injustice in the world and set out to help in whatever way he could. Simple as that, and yet most people don't put in the effort. It was while watching him that I realized I wanted the same thing for my life. I sailed with him for twenty years, Daava. If I told you all the adventures we had, I might be speaking for weeks on end."

"I would like to hear them," his father said, wistful wonder pursing his mouth.

"I'll share them in time, but for now, I think I should move on to the next shift in my journey. That time Ulio invited me for yet another drink in the cabin of his ship. And yet somehow I knew it would not just be another drink. I could see it in his eyes, hear it in his tone. I already guessed a little of what he had to say, but I was not prepared for the full of it."

THE CRIMSON CRANE

PAST

"Take a seat, lad," Ulio said. He held his most prized and rare flagon of sake, something Coren had only seen him pull from his top shelf one other time. As Coren took the seat across from him, he filled both mugs, the ice chips inside tinkling like little bells.

By now, Coren knew he didn't get drunk easily so he took a sip from the proffered cup without concern. As for the captain, the man's constitution seemed to defy something as weak as drunkenness.

"It's been quite the life, hasn't it?" Ulio rumbled.

"Aye." Coren swallowed, the sweet sting of the flavor reflecting the pain that was beginning to kindle in his heart. He knew where this conversation was headed, he'd known the moment he stepped in.

"I'm getting too old for sailing to and fro, you know."

"Are you?" Coren asked innocently, never mind that the man had been silver-haired since before they'd met.

Ulio chuckled. "Don't give me that face, ya little sea sprite. It's time I retired and let someone new take over. I've been thinking about it for years. I just never could bring myself to do it, because I was always...always afraid that if I stopped, so would everything else. That there would be no one to continue the work. Some of my best mates are not much younger than I, so I knew there was no point asking them. Wasn't sure what I would do. And then came you. You bright-eyed, reckless ginger. Honestly, your fire is what kept me going these past few years. And now I know you're the one. You're the one to inherit my ship."

Coren's mouth dropped open. Inherit the mission, yes, he understood why the man would ask him to do that, but to give him his ship, his beloved *Crimson Crane*, was another matter entirely.

"You know the business with Dormandy. You can keep that up or start something new if you wish. Whatever you end up doing, I want you to succeed. And that is why I am giving you the fruits of my labor. The fortune I have gathered from the success of my business and the treasure I have found from my adventures. It is a small fortune, but a fortune fit to keep you afloat. You won't need to write home for help anyway."

"That's always a good thing," Coren managed to say with a small laugh, but his throat was dry. He'd known the man long enough to know that he'd be a wise saver of his money as well as a charitable giver. But now it seemed he'd intended to give away all of it. "What...what about your retirement though?"

"What about it? Never mind, lad, I'll keep enough to live comfortably to the end of my days, but sleeping on a bed of gold won't do much for these aching bones. Better to pass the fortune on to one who can use it, and use it well."

"But where will you go? What will you do?"

"Can't see me sitting still, can you? Cooped up in some salt-crusted shack in Dormandy's port? I've asked myself the same, you know. This is my life's work, but I took no wife, fathered no children. No family for me in my final days, is that on your mind?"

Coren flinched, the sorrow in his eyes deepening.

But Ulio's brilliant smile spread wide across his face once more. "Do not fret, lad. I'm going to the islands, and I will live out the rest of my days in Kuah's village. I'll sit on those warm sands and drink those sweet fruits and when I see the children and the grandchildren of those people whose lives I've returned play at my feet, I will think, 'here, they are free.' And that will be all the happiness I could ever want." His eyes filled with sudden tears as he spoke and he swiped a hand across his face to cover a hastily contrived cough.

"I know you will carry on the work, Coren. I've lived my dream. Now make it your own. When a ship starts a new life, she needs a new name. You'll have to think on that one, but make it good."

"The *Solitary Star*." He spoke the name without hesitation. He'd dreamed of the day he'd get his own ship, so of course he'd already thought of names. In the end, there had really only been one choice. One that reflected himself. He just had never dreamed that the ship he so loved would become his own.

A twinkle shimmered in Ulio's eyes. "So she is. So she is," he said. "And she's all yours, Captain Coren."

OOLUM

Present

Leoren leaned back in his chair, stretching his arms out in front of him, brow furrowed in reflection. "So if you were contracted under Dormandy and sailing to the Southern Sea, how did you end up as an Oolum merchant vessel?"

"Aye, how did I?" Coren muttered, climbing back up from the cellar he'd vanished in a few minutes ago, a few cakes wrapped in paper now in his hands. He tore off the wrapping as he considered the question. "Well, the truth is, I kept feeling a pull to the Eastern shores and her cities. Ulio had taken me there a few times in our travels, and I fell in love with the culture and the people. But even as I was enchanted by the sights and smells, I was also taken aback at how little they esteemed life and how easily they just bought and sold each other.

"It was quite a thing, the first slave auction I saw. There were several children that day, and sadder, emptier faces I never did see. I often dreamed of those people who had no hand and no law to help them. Prevention was a great thing, but there were now other ships that took the Dormandy contract for hunting slavers whether for the pay or because they had a similar drive—some even had sailed with Ulio and been inspired to set a course in his wake. There was no one, as far as I knew, who was actually going to where the slaves already existed and trying to set them free. It was dangerous and foolish, most thought, sticking your nose into that kind of business. But it wouldn't leave my mind.

"Still, I knew I couldn't just sail into port in those waters and not have my red sails recognized. When in trading docks, the pirates or slavers might stay clear of causing trouble, but they would know my ship's reputation. So I traded out her red sails for white."

The decision had hurt. He'd loved those brilliant red sails more than he could express, but he didn't suppose saying as much would convey the feeling to his father.

In addition to the change of sails, the change of the ship's name and ownership helped prevent being recognized on paper.

"Your sails are red now," Leoren observed.

"It is amazing how quickly humans forget!" Coren threw back his head with a laugh. "After about seven years, I put the red sails on again, and while a few looks were sent my way, I was already known as a reliable merchant, and I was clearly no Ulio, who had been just as much a legend as the red sails."

"Anyway," he continued, "I kept a pretty low profile for my first two years in Oolum. I just did simple trade routes back and forth, making acquaintances, building relationships, earning a trusted reputation, helping out those struggling with life, that sort of thing."

"And then you met Zizain," Leoren said, his mouth curling in the smug smile of one who already knows the plot twist.

"Yes." Coren grinned. "And then I met Zizain."

8

OOLUM

Past

The taverns in Oolum were fashioned to accommodate various guests from all over the world according to their customs. The locals did business with each other in private homes over finely brewed tea or coffee, but they had also built inns similar to those on the western shore to sell drink and board to the visiting sailors and merchants.

And there were times it paid to look like some common Dormandy sailor just sitting down for a drink between voyages. The people who had lived generations in Oolum tended to speak freely in their native tongue, assuming they could not be understood. Coren had avoided a few bad trade deals, even assaults, by learning every language he came across.

The men in the table behind him were bartering over something. He heard only bits of it with one ear. The other ear was tuned to the chatter about the tavern. The clink of pewter, a belch, something about somebody's mother, the squawk of a chicken just outside, and always the harsh laughter and barking voices.

Hold it.

The surrounding cacophony dimmed instantly as all his attention turned to the conversation behind him.

He turned in his seat, overlooking the wooden booth to see past the shoulders and heads of the talking men. Facing him sat one young man and a younger woman. The girl's face was slack in shock.

Shock that she'd just been included as the prize for whatever trade they were making.

The man she was with could have just picked her up off the street, but there was something in how she looked at him that spoke complete betrayal. A family member perhaps? No. A lover, if the way his arm clung around her shoulders was any indication. Whatever his relation, it didn't matter.

Coren stood. Walked around to face their table. "Afternoon, lads," he said in perfect Oolumeese, jarring their conversation. "Couldn't help but overhear the little trade deal you're discussing."

Several pairs of eyes narrowed in a glare. "It's none of your business," the young man said.

"I'm making it my business," Coren replied. "Nasty thing, dealing in human lives, you know."

"Shove off, west rat," another man sneered, blackened gums showing. "There is no law against it in these lands."

"Oh, there's a law." Coren crossed his arms. "You just haven't heard of it, I wager."

"And what are you going to do? Call authorities?"

"Heaven, no," Coren chuckled. "Why would they even care? Everyone knows that fights just happen in a bar."

He kicked the table, sending it flipping and scattering mugs of ale at shrieking customers. Before the table had finished clattering on the ground, he reached out, wrenched the girl out of the man's arms and set her behind him. He turned back just in time to catch an incoming fist.

"Banu!" he shouted as he swerved to the side, pulling the man forward and driving his knee up into his bent stomach. "Come and chat with this girl for me, won't you?"

He didn't need to look to know that the bar woman serving up the drinks would already be heading over and she would pull the girl away from the fight until it was finished. Banu was in her sixties and well-acquainted with tavern brawls. In the few years Coren had spent here, they'd secured a sort of understanding when it came to fights that he found himself involved in. He'd take responsibility for any messes. As for Banu herself, she was an esteemed tavern owner whose word could stop a fight in an instant. Men wouldn't argue, not even the new ones. She wasn't somebody anyone tried to include in a tussle. Mainly out of respect, but also because there was some fear that she might break all your bones.

Coren felt the wind of someone leaping at him from behind, and he ducked. The man staggered, his target suddenly gone. Coren reached up, grabbed his collar, and threw him the rest of the way over, his back smacking into the floor with the force of the somersault. Another man, just charging, stumbled over the body of the first. They cursed and spluttered as they tried to untangle themselves, glaring at Coren as he lightly took a few steps back, still poised to fight. It was then that the men seemed to notice that the one young man—the very one who had offered the girl in the deal—had already run out the door, leaving both them and the girl behind.

"I believe we could call this matter concluded, lads," Coren said, bouncing on his toes. "Unless you like brawling. I do. I think it's fun."

The men glowered, but they stumbled to their feet and stalked past him, giving him a wide berth, as they headed for the door. They didn't glance at anyone else, they just left.

"Didn't even offer to pay for their drinks and food," Banu grumbled, her arm wrapped protectively around the young woman.

"I was the one who smashed it all on the floor," Coren said, digging into his pouch and pulling out a small coin purse. "Sorry for the trouble, Banu."

The young woman, still and rigid as a hunted rabbit, looked back and forth between them. The shock-struck glaze to her eyes was beginning to fade, replaced by an irritated and ferocious gleam. "What is this all about?" she finally snapped. Her voice was thick with the Oolum accent, rolling with a rich umber tone and crisply sharp at the edges.

"I rather thought you didn't want to be traded off to his thug friends?" Coren replied, raising a brow. "Either way, I didn't want you to be."

"So, so, hero," she said, rolling her eyes. "You want my thanks?" She shrugged her arm, pulling free of Banu's light grasp and took a step towards the door.

Coren intercepted her, not minding that it earned him another suspicious glare. She was free to think him a villain with his own ends all she liked, but that didn't change what he had to do. "Where are you headed now?" he asked. "Back to him?" He knew how it went by now. They almost always went back.

"What if I am?" The 'z' lisp to her words was more cutting than ever.

"Why?" He kept the anger out of his voice, because it wasn't for her. It was for the whole vicious cycle that kept victims trapped. "Why would you return to him? Is this his first time trying to sell you? Or his tenth? He'll just keep doing it once he starts. You know you don't want that."

"He wasn't going to!" she said, eyes flashing up to glare at him. "He just said that so we could get the money we needed."

"Sure. Sure. He wouldn't really do that because he says things like 'I love you,' doesn't he? And even if he went through with the deal, it would be all right because he has his reasons, doesn't he?" Coren sighed, rubbing the edge of his finger down the bridge of his nose. Back when he was younger, it had seemed so foolish to him, this idea of staying with someone harmful out of desperation to be loved. He wasn't sure he understood it even now, but he was familiar with the pattern. "Look.

Don't go back to him right now. Banu will give you a room and a meal for tonight. Think it over."

Banu didn't question who would pay for that, she just held her hand out expectantly and Coren flipped another small purse of coins from his pouch to her hand.

"You clean up this mess, eh?" she barked, before turning a gentler smile to the girl. "You come with me, lamb, we will find you some dates to eat." One did not simply refuse Banu, so the girl followed her to the stairs, and Coren's mind could rest easy for the moment that she would not be running right back into danger.

The racket of the tavern, only briefly interrupted by the short fight, had swung back into rhythm, and people were already stepping in the puddles of spilled ale. He swiped a rag and bucket from behind the counter and set it in the middle of the mess, then grabbed the table and flipped it right side up. Finding the mugs took a bit longer, especially since someone had kicked one underneath another table.

The girl wouldn't stay here long. He knew he couldn't talk her out of staying away from that man.

The man, however, was another matter.

There were times it paid to look like nothing more than a shadow on the sand. His clothes were neither dark nor light, just deep grey. Not black enough to stand out against the pale walls, not bright enough to reflect the occasional torch. His head and hands were likewise wrapped in the same fabric after the style of the traders who took long roads through the desert. So he slipped without pause from street to street, taking short-cuts across the rooftops or the edge of fences when he wished.

Osar. That was the name Banu had given him. With that name, he'd tracked down a few others—namely, the quarter and street in which he lived.

The man was stumbling about, the drunkenness of his activities catching up with him. Good. He hadn't gone to bed yet. As a whole, Coren disliked breaking into houses.

He dropped from the roof to the sand without even a whisper of sound. Not that the man would have noticed even if he'd come crashing down. Clearing his throat, he tapped the man on the shoulder.

When the man turned, he wasn't there.

He turned with him, stepping behind his shoulder again.

"Osar," he whispered.

The man jerked, spinning. Coren revolved with him, always one step out of sight. As the man looked about in confusion, he reached out, caught him at the base of the neck, and pushed him into the wall.

Osar yelped and flailed. "Ei! Ei, I'll pay you back, I swear, I swear!"

How many bad deals and false promises had this miserable creature made? "I am not here for that," Coren said, voice soft and flat. "I am here about the girl. You will neither speak to her nor touch her ever again. If you see her, you run. Perhaps out of the very city."

"What?" The man warbled in confusion.

Coren's grip tightened, not enough to hurt, but enough to remind that he meant business. "You heard what I said. You know what I mean. I am letting you go, but I will watch you. I will watch from your shadow. I will watch from the dark. You betrayed the trust of somebody who thought you cared. In that, you betray yourself. Choose differently from now on, lest you hang from a noose of your own making."

OOLUM

Present

"Stars," Leoren exclaimed. "I didn't know you could be terrifying. If I didn't know better, I would say you learned from Cerand."

"Thank you," Coren said, with a slight bow. "I'll take that as the highest of praise."

"Poor Zizain," Leoren shook his head, lips pressed together in displeasure with the awfulness of the world. "That was Zizain, wasn't it?"

"I suppose we shall have to continue if you want to find out."

9

OOLUM

Past

A line of people stretched down the street and around the corner, coming empty-handed and then trailing back with a bit of food like little ants. Bags of dry beans, barley, and packets of salted fish had been packed tight into crates, but the resources were dwindling, and Coren knew they would run out before everyone could be fed. He hated whenever it came to that, hated the looks of disappointment and fear. Honestly, it paid to have his sailors around, both to keep order in the lines and to discourage any kind of uproar. But he needed to do more. He could only buy so many crates for so long without draining his own ability to keep serving.

Perhaps if he approached some of the business owners in Dormandy and Oolum about donating some portions of food shipments as part of his payment for carrying their loads across the gulf...there were a few who were religious or superstitious enough to be talked into charity if they thought it would benefit their eternal souls. Maybe a few would even do it out of the sincerity of their heart.

He handed another bag and packet to the person waiting in front of him, but they didn't reach to take it. Instead, they just stood there, staring at him. His eyes focused, recognizing the small figure.

"You..." he said in surprise. "You're that girl." The young woman from the tavern. Banu had said she'd disappeared the following morning without a word, and he'd figured that was the last he'd see of her in a city this size.

"And you're that man," she said, not a bit surprised and wearing a smug grin. Had she been looking for him on purpose? "So is this what you do for a living? Pawn off your shipments to the street rats? Won't your superiors complain?"

"Everything here is paid for fair and square, miss, don't you worry about that. Now do you want some or not?" She was here without that scum of a fellow, so that was good news. And her expression was without anguish or fear, so that was better.

She stepped out of line, letting the next person hurry forward and snatch the bags out of Coren's hand and then rush on to the next sailor who distributed the kegs of lemon water. Standing to Coren's left, she watched in silence for a few minutes as he hurried to keep up with the rush of the crowd. After a few moments, she reached into the crate holding the packets of salted fish, sniffed it, and then handed it to the next approaching woman with a friendly smile.

"Hang on, what are you doing?" Coren said, lifting his head out of the crate as he dug for the bottom bags.

"Helping. You got something against it?"

"Not at all, it's just—" Why? Well, there was no point in asking now. There was too much to do, no time to just pause and chat. If she wanted to help, fine. Maybe she wanted to earn some coin. He could pay her in that case, once the crowds had gone.

It didn't take long to go through the remaining rations. When he announced the end to the dismay of the line, it took several more minutes to answer questions about when the supplies would be replenished and where they might find him next. Several folk lingered about to eye the empty crates as if to be sure he wasn't hiding more.

More. He wished. He wished there could be more. Sometimes he was tempted to just bleed himself dry. But even then it wouldn't be enough to meet the need. He needed a plan for the long-term.

The sun was beginning to set, the sailors were lifting the crates back onto the wagons, when suddenly the girl was in front of him again. He'd lost track of her somewhere in the commotion and figured she'd gone home.

"Not everybody in that line deserved the food, you know," she said, raising a brow.

"Probably, but not my place to judge," Coren said. "There were a lot of women and children and crippled, so that's what's important."

"You new here?" she asked. "I would have heard about some charitable do-gooder. I've lived on the streets all my life."

"I've been coming in and out of Oolum, but yes, this is a more recent development. I've been trying to meet needs on a smaller scale, but decided to try expanding. Why, do you need some help?"

Her brown eyes narrowed. "Just passing out food for free. That gets around. What are you planning to do about the robbers? You got your crew, and they look like a mongrel bunch, but you sure they can keep you safe?"

His chest tightened. He knew that. Of course, he knew that. The world wasn't a place where you could give things away without people trying to take it from you by force. He and his crew would anchor out from the harbor at night, and a constant guard was kept. "What's your point?"

"I think you need my help." She flicked her long brown hair over her shoulder. "You've been here, what, a year? Two years? That's nothing compared to a little rat born from the sand. I know these streets, I know these people."

"So you're looking for a job. Sorry, I don't take girls on my voyages." Not unless he was smuggling someone to safety, but even with the level of faith he held in his crew, he didn't fancy mixing women and sailors.

She spat to the side. "Like I want to be stuck on a boat with filthy men. I am talking about here, silly coppertop. I can be your contact on the streets. I can be your ears and eyes."

He had a few of those already, but more certainly would not hurt. Hefting the last crate onto the wagon, he turned against it and wiped the sweat from his brow. Taking the leather flask from his waist, he handed it over to her. "So what's your name?"

"Zizain." The name sparkled with the same mischievous glint as the gold in her eyes.

"Do you have any family, Zizain?" he questioned.

"No." She sniffed at the flask and then gulped a few swallows down.

"What happened to them?"

She peered at him over the rim of the flask as if she thought it strange he would even question their absence. "Never knew my da. Mami disappeared when I was eight."

"And you've been on your own ever since?" Until she ran into Osar.

Her mouth twitched, that bright glint of smile showing ever so slightly. "So what if I have? Same as a lot of folks around here. What about you, aren't you on your own?"

"Well, I mean...I have family. It's just been a while, so...more or less." Wait, how did this get turned on him? He sighed and shook his head. "Fine, then. You're hired. I often go to Banu's inn, so you can find me there. Part of your payment will be coin, part of it will be food. How about that?"

"Aye, Cap'n." She drew herself into the laziest salute he ever did see and flashed him another wink.

Coren rolled his eyes. *Celestial saints, what have I roped myself into?*

He'd bought a small house in Oolum. The Merchant Quarter, where you could keep a simple square building of sandstone to guard your wares when you weren't selling them. There was not much in it besides a bed, a larder, and a few cupboards. The houses were cheap enough, provided you had the papers to prove you were a merchant. Normally, he would have just slept on his ship, but he wished to know the city better, and so had taken to living here in between routes.

Still, he was getting enough attention from the locals not to wish for them to know exactly where he lived, so before heading home, he'd duck into a dark corner in some secluded alley, and wrap himself in a long tunic and head shawl, before setting out again.

Only once he was home, he shrugged off the quick disguise. The streets were fairly quiet in this part of town, except for the occasional man bidding the day farewell in a throaty, reverent song. It did not matter if the fellow merchants saw him here or not, and it wasn't as if he had visitors anyway.

Or, normally, he did not have visitors.

"So this is where you live, eh? Here I thought you slept on your boat all the time."

Coren whirled, hand on his knife hilt, even though his brain was scrambling to remind him that he knew that voice and it was harmless even if it did *not* belong here.

Sure enough, there she stood. Hands on her hips, big, brown eyes appraising his living space with curiosity.

"How did you—" he began.

"Told you, Cap'n, I was bred and born in this city, I know it upside down and inside out. Clever of you to change your clothes, but you weren't completely hidden, by the way, not from above."

Trying not to feel unnerved that he'd been watched all that time, he gave a shrug of his shoulder. "Alright, fine. This is where I live. Not that you needed to know. Is there something else you need?"

"Bold of you to assume it is I who am the one in need." She padded about the house on bare feet, examining the sparse shelves, lifting the rug to find the hatch to his larder, poking the thin mattress on the wooden bench in the corner. "Seems to me that you're the one in need of a house-guard."

"No thieves if there's nothing to steal," Coren pointed out.

"So you say." She plopped down on crossed legs beside the door and settled comfortably against the wall, very much like a cat claiming its favorite spot in the sun.

"Hold on just a minute." Coren set his hands on his hips. "You're not staying here, if that's what you think. If you are looking for a place to stay, I can take you back to Banu and pay for another night."

"You going to pick me up and throw me out?" Her brows rose in challenge, mouth turning up in a smirk at his expression of annoyance. "No? That's what I thought."

Silver saints in the heavens, what was he supposed to do? It was out of the question to let her stay, wasn't it?

Turning away to gather his bearings, he knelt down to open the hatch with the key he kept around his neck and descended into his cellar. A moment in the cold dark was what he needed to clear his head, yes, that was it. He didn't keep much food on hand, preferring to buy it as needed, but he found some dried fruits and wax-papered cheese.

So what if she did stay? It wasn't as if she actually had anything to fear from him. On the contrary, perhaps the reason she wanted to stay was because she knew it was safer here. Should he offer her his bed? No, it wasn't like he wished to encourage her to hang around. But he grabbed another blanket and climbed back up the ladder.

She sat where he'd left her, basking in the amber sunset glow peeking through the cracked door. One eye peeled open as he tossed the blanket and a package of the cheese and fruit onto her lap.

"Since you're already here, you can stay," he said, not looking her in the face. "Just don't plan on making it a habit." Without waiting for a response, he headed for his cot, pulled off his boots, and flipped his face to the corner.

He doubted he was going to sleep tonight.

And then he woke up, squinting at the bit of light shafting into the room from the opposite direction as before. Morning. Morning already? He didn't even remember drifting off. The girl had kept silent, not disturbing his slumber in the slightest. His face was turned towards the door, having rolled over sometime in the night, and he lifted himself onto one elbow and squinted into the shadows of his house.

No, she was definitely gone. Just as well. Even so, he felt a twinge of regret. Living on the streets had to be tough. There wasn't much to stop any burglars or evil-doers from coming through the door if they wanted, but still a door, four walls, and a roof was often enough to deter them as opposed to someone just sleeping out in the open.

Levering himself to his feet, he adjusted the belt at his waist and rubbed the sore spot where the knife hilt had dug into his ribs. Usually, he'd have taken it off during the night and slept with it by his side. For that matter, he would have taken off his shirt too. But Zizain's presence had eliminated those normal habits from his routine. Now that she had left, he opened a drawer in his only cupboard and pulled out a fresh shirt.

Breakfast first. He'd go down to the wharf, buy a fresh fish, and cook it on the public fires. Talk to the sailors, maybe take a new commission for a merchant seeking to trade overseas.

Tugging the new shirt over his head, he stepped out the door. In this city there were only a few moments in a day when the air was cool, light, and fresh. He could still smell the salt and grime, but there was something else in each breath, some promise of new life. A solemnness weighted the atmosphere, hushing the sounds of carts and shouts, listening instead to a deep hum upon the wind—the sound of a thousand voices lifted up in their morning hymn as many citizens of Oolum would stand on their roof to welcome the day in song. He closed his eyes, listening to the sound, feeling the breeze upon his skin, smelling the—

—smelling the cake? Most houses in these quarters were not built with the intention to vent smoke, so they baked outside in a little pit beside the stoop. The crackle of fire drew Coren's attention down to his, where a little skillet rested on the ember-bright rocks, a flat dough bubbling up into a crust upon its surface. And beside that fire and that skillet crouched Zizain.

"The sun rises again today!" she greeted cheerfully.

"Um." Coren took a step backwards.

"That is not the traditional response. Though I can see why you'd be surprised."

He looked back in the way he'd come, then back at her, then further down the street. "I thought you'd left. Wait. Where did you get those ingredients?"

"Your larder."

"But I—" His hand darted to his neck, but before he'd even finished searching, he had his answer.

Zizain dangled the twine necklace from her fingers, keys hanging on the end. "You sleep deeper than you should, sailor man. But you don't snore. I must commend you for that."

So much for the legendary alertness of his elven blood. He reached for the key and she gave it back without fuss. Honestly, he wasn't sure what to think. At the very least, it proved she wasn't going to murder him in his sleep, not that he'd been much worried about that to begin with.

She scraped the hotcakes from the pan with a piece of shingle and tossed him one. He caught it, bouncing it from finger to finger, and blowing off the heat. When he took a bite, the fluffy texture burst into the flavor of honey and oil. Something else too. Cardamom? He was pretty sure he had not stored all the ingredients needed in his larder, which meant either the coin purse at his waist was a few coins short or she'd used the wages he'd given her yesterday.

"It's good," he said, trying not to suggest how long it had been since he'd bothered to make himself homemade hotcakes. Somehow, it suddenly reminded him of home, even if they made them with different ingredients and sweet sauces there. But yet everything tasted better out here, perhaps in contrast with the difficulty of living.

"Bet you thought I just ate scraps and didn't know how to cook something nice," she said, jutting out her chin. "Osar and I used to snatch vials of saffron and rosewater to make our own desserts. He had an incurable sweet tooth, so I'd—" She broke off, eyes widening as if it just struck her who she was talking about.

Coren watched her from the corner of his eye as she struggled to steady the sudden tremble in her chin, her throat striving to swallow a lump.

Wiping off his mouth, he pulled a few coins from his waist and rubbed them together. "Now that we've had our sweets, how do you feel about some roasted fish to give us strength for the day?"

Her eyes brightened with a light other than tears. "Fresh caught?" She grabbed the small pot of water by her feet and doused it over the glowing coals, a hiss rising from the rocks.

"Pulled straight out of the sea." He flicked his head. "It's how I normally start my day, and seeing how you are still here, I figured you'd just invite yourself along if I didn't invite you first."

She smiled, brushing the flour off her hands. "You catch on quick, Cap'n."

10

OOLUM

Present

"**I** take it she never left your side after that," Leoren said, mouth twitching in a soft smile.

"Not for any extended periods of time, no."

"When did she come to share your faith in Ayeshune? I'm assuming she wasn't already a believer in His grace?"

"Well, by following me everywhere, she ended up following me to my times of prayer or when I gathered with those of faith. It didn't take her very long to declare belief, though I think it took a bit longer to actually mean it. She already knew some things about Ayeshune, but in Oolum and other parts of the East, he is known as the Old God."

"Old God?" Leoren's brows shot up. "That makes him sound decrepit."

"Well, to follow their logic, I suppose there is no one older. Even so, I too found it a bit amusing at first. It is strange how quickly human culture changes compared to the elves."

"Speaking of that." Taking another sip of the turmeric tea, he gave a nod to Coren's ears. "When did she find out you were an elf?"

Coren gave an embarrassed chuckle, hand ruffling the back of his hair. "Oh, that. Yes. I should have told her. But she sort of…found out. It was about two years after I met her. A sickness had broken out in Oolum, and it was spreading like fire through the poverty-stricken streets. You remember how Tellie said her parents were taken by a sickness called the Flags?"

"Yes."

"Same plague, different place. Over in the east, we called it Red Fever." He rubbed a hand down the skin of his arm, imagining the horror of it all over again.

11

OOLUM

Past

D ays like this made Coren wish he'd spent more time at the Healing House of Damarik. That is, time that wasn't spent waiting for a broken bone to be set or a deep gash to be stitched after a wild day out in the woods. The healer and his entire family were quiet people, very detailed in everything they did, and thus he had found them rather slow and boring as a child. But their tutelage would have been invaluable in the circumstances he found himself in now.

Even so, that which he did know from elvish living and his own experiences out in the world left him feeling more prepared than most when the sickness took root in the streets of Oolum. Sickness thrived in the gutters, and therein lay his first challenge. Cleanliness.

The first thing he bought was a warehouse. A thick stone building with a few windows near the roof so that the inside was kept cool. He sectioned it into rooms with sheets hung on poles and had mats rolled out onto the hard floor. It was packed now with the sick, coughs and groans echoing up to the ceiling.

The warehouse had been a bargain buy, but the real expenses came from buying the linens, the medicinal herbs, and the materials to make soap. Mainly just oil for the latter; he tried to cut cost by making his own ash from wood.

At least money was still coming from his merchant trade, along with some supplies from benefactors. Indeed, the *Solitary Star* seemed to be cutting across the waters more often than ever in her quest to bring supplies to the ravaged city. On the other hand, exports from Oolum had all but ceased as nobody wished to catch the outbreak of plague. The sailors delivered the goods, but did very little to mix in with the crowds.

Hence why Coren was here on the sand instead of out on the sea. He'd left his ship to the command of his first mate almost as soon as the Red Fever had emerged. He'd known where he would be most needed.

Of course, right now, there was nowhere he'd rather be than on the waves with a cool breeze on his skin and fresh air filling his lungs.

Wait, scratch that. He wished he could be back in Aselvia on a rainy day. Yes, one of those misty mornings where the fog was coming through the thickets.

The soft moan of a little child brought his mind back to reality, back to the *reason* he was here instead of there. The small girl lying before him was covered with the splotchy red rash that accompanied this fever. He dipped another rag into the pot of water by his knee, spread it over her skin, and then grabbed a piece of parchment and started waving it vigorously above her body. The water was warm, and ice was as coveted as diamonds during this time, so this was the best he could do at keeping her cool.

He was so tired of this sickness. Even when he closed his eyes, the pattern of the rash would dance against the darkness.

The child's mother gave a slight cough, and Coren eyed her with concern. So far her body seemed to be tolerating the sickness, but they would have to keep a close eye on that.

"Coren." Zizain appeared at his side. Her usual colorful garb was replaced with a sleeveless flax tunic, darkened with the sweat of her work. Pretty clothes and such luxuries had quickly been exchanged for just the necessities to survive this plague. A yoke hung across her shoulders, balanced on either end by two clay vessels of water. Freshwater was hard to come by in this city. Right now, the lines to the public wells could take hours.

"Oh good, you're back," Coren started to push himself up. It didn't quite work.

"You all right?" Her tone sharpened.

"Just a bit dizzy with all this heat. Let's get that water cleaned and cooled. I've got these cloths to wash anyway." He took hold of the basket of linens and pushed himself to his feet with better success.

"Coren, hold on."

"Tell me as we go, Zi, tell me as we go." There was a backroom where he kept cauldrons full of water boiling over fires. Some of it was saltwater, and that he kept for cleaning or for steaming into freshwater. The other was well-water. Both had to be boiled to kill whatever filth lingered within, but it made the room incredibly hot and heavy.

"Coren, will you just slow down?" Zizain's voice peppered his back like bits of shale. "I'm trying to tell you to get some rest and you won't even stop to hear that!"

"Never mind me, Zizain," Coren called back over his shoulder, not breaking stride. "I have more strength than you know. I can't stop, there aren't enough of us. If anyone should take a break, it's you after bringing in the water." He shoved open the heavy door to the boiler room with his shoulder, staggering a bit under the weight of the basket of linens he carried. The oppressive heat slammed into his face, adding another few coats of sweat onto his skin. Honestly, he was sure any sickness would have to be drowning in this amount of perspiration. He bent over to set the basket upon the ground, and in the moment that blood rushed to his head, he knew—he wasn't all right, after all.

The world tilted, then went dark.

The trickle of water running down his temple and neck was the next thing he was aware of. He lay there for a bit, trying to get a sense of his surroundings, but even though his head felt stuffed with cotton, his thoughts spun away every time he reached for them. So instead, he listened, waiting for any sound that would ground him in reality. He heard distant shouting, so he was in a house somewhere behind a closed door. He heard the swish of a rag being wrung of water, the droplets returning to a bowl in a tinkling melody. Finally, he forced his eyes open, blinking away the crust clinging to his lashes. The stone roof filling his gaze was a bit fuzzy, and it took a while to bring it into focus.

His skin itched. All over.

He raised one hand before his face and wondered why his vision was still so blotchy. Blotchy red even.

Oh.

Hand falling listlessly back to his chest, he craned his neck to the side and found the source of the sounds of water. Zizain sat cross-legged next to him, cleaning a rag in the bowl set in her lap.

"Hey," he whispered softly, voice rough and weak.

Her shoulders jumped and she nearly fell over in her haste to face him. "You're awake!" she exclaimed, brightness entering her dark eyes, chasing away the dullness that had filmed their surface a moment before.

"I guess...I got the sickness," he said.

"You think?" She shook her head and returned to throttling the rag. No more water was coming out, so she dipped it before twisting again. "Why didn't you tell me?" Her words were chipped, angry.

"Zi, I didn't even know, I was just too busy—"

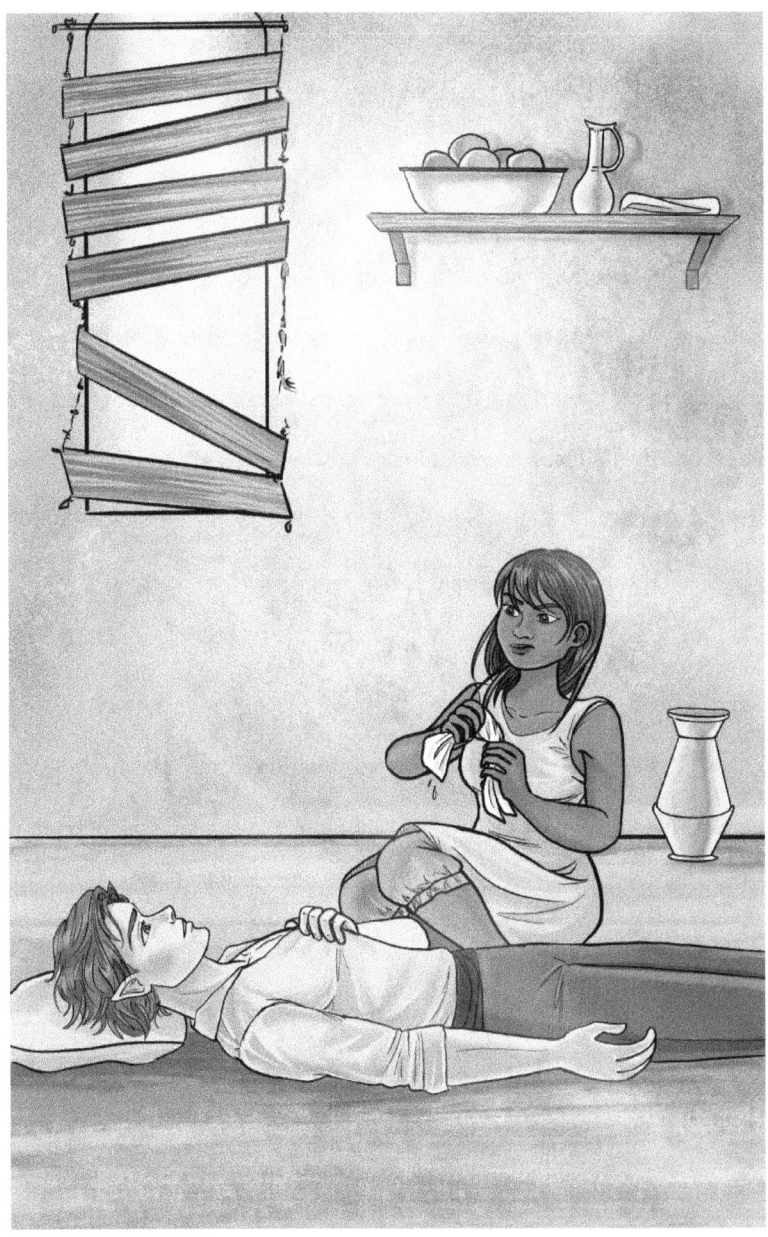

"Not the fever, idiot." She reached over and gave his ears a sharp tug. "Why didn't you tell me about this?"

His mind went blank.

That.

Of course, she would have noticed if she'd been caring for him the past few days. His wild hair kept the tips covered and people didn't usually look for something they were not expecting to see. They were not as especially pointy as others of his race, which was a blessing, but there was no mistaking it when observed closely.

He probably should have told her before now.

"Can it wait?" he asked, allowing himself to sound as pathetic as he felt.

"I," she said, punctuating the word with a jab to his chest, "have been waiting for the past two days. I'd like an explanation this instant."

"Well," he said slowly, trying to gather his thoughts. "I'm an elf."

"I figured that part out, you dolt."

"You could have thought I was a chema. Pointy ears and all that."

"I've seen the occasional chema, their ears are entirely different," she said with a snort. "Why are you out here all alone, pretending to be human?"

"Never said I was a human," he murmured.

"Never said you weren't, either," she said, poking him again.

"I'm feeling very attacked for a sick person."

"Keep talking."

He heaved a gusty sigh. "I just…it's easier this way to avoid unwanted attention. The things we do, Zizain, I don't want it about me. Elves are reclusive and famed enough that I'd get swamped with every kind of interest. So, I don't tell many people. It's not important."

"Oh, good to know that it wasn't important for me to know, not your partner of two years!"

Comparatively, that was less time than some people he knew who still had no clue, but he supposed she wouldn't appreciate that detail right now.

"I'm sorry," he whispered.

"Sorry," she huffed. Dousing the rag again, she ran its coolness over his brow. The scrunch in her nose softened. "I won't tell a soul," she said. "Don't worry about that. You just get better, you hear?"

He nodded, eyes already closing with heaviness. The soft swish of the rag and the low hum in her throat soon lulled him to sleep.

OOLUM

Present

"How long did it take you to recover?" Leoren asked, tone troubled at the idea of his son off somewhere dying of sickness whilst he'd been sipping tea in Aselvia.

"Another few days or so before I was on my feet. Zizain scolded me, said I needed to rest longer, but there was just so much to be done, and I knew I was on the mend. It took many more months before the intensity of the plague faded. So many died. So many. Not because the sickness couldn't be beat, but because there just weren't enough people helping them in their need." He sighed, taking a sip of water to ease his dry throat.

"Did Zizain treat you any differently once she knew you were an elf?"

"Oh yes. Yes, she did."

12

OOLUM

Past

Now that she knew, her questions were about Aselvia and elves in general whenever they had a moment alone. For the most part, Coren found them extremely petty questions. Things like "if the men grow their hair long, how come yours is short?" and "is it true hair only grows on your head? I always wondered how you found time to wax so often," and "are the women all very beautiful?"

After his careless confirmation of the latter question, she had gone silent for a few minutes, before a new one raised its insistent flag. "Is that why you've never given me a look over? Am I too below you?"

He paused in reading the ledger of goods he'd been looking over. Now was really not the time to try and figure out paperwork. "Brights, Zizain, where'd you get an idea like that? Can't it just be that maybe I respect God and women?"

"Men say that, don't mean it," she said matter-of-factly. "But I guess you're not a man."

"I'm a man, Zi," he said in exasperation. "Just not a *hu*-man."

"So all elves are saints, eh? No wandering eye among 'em? How do you end up having any kids?"

He rolled his eyes. "Hardly saints. And fine, if you want a biological explanation, elves don't have many children because elvish women only can be with child every ten years. As such we are just a bit differently designed than humans, so our minds aren't as given over to lust. It doesn't mean it's impossible."

Perhaps he shouldn't have added that last bit, because a spark of a challenge lit in her eyes. But instead she asked, "So what sins are elves prone to?"

"Gossip," he answered immediately. "Long lives where everyone knows everyone, gossip is as thick there as the flies are here."

"What's wrong with a juicy gab?"

"Well, you have to admit it doesn't usually spread good feelings."

She conceded that with a shrug of her shoulder and then marched straight ahead with her questions. "What else?"

"Pride...a long memory...combining the two makes for some deep grudges. Hard to let go." In a way, he couldn't blame his people because of what they'd experienced, but...it had been hundreds of years ago, the humans who had done them wrong were dead, and it was time to move on and try again. And yet...and yet, he had a grudge of his own. That little voice that whispered he hadn't forgiven his parents. His father. That the real reason he was staying away was not because he was worried about Zizain but because he was glad to have a reason not to visit.

"So what about your family?"

"Huh?"

"You've got one, don't you?"

She had to ask that just as he was thinking about his father...

"Um. Yes. Parents."

"Aye, and? Do they have names? Things they do other than sit around and look pretty?"

When he spoke of life back home with anyone, which was rare, he had never been particularly detailed about the circumstances into which he was born. It was enough that someone knew he was an elf, they didn't need to know he was a prince on top of it. But somehow Zizain's hurt about his keeping secrets had stung deeper than he realized, for he found himself opening his mouth and saying, "My father works as an ambassador. My mother was the sister of the late queen, and she takes care of her mother who is ill."

"Fancy!" Zizain said. "Doesn't that make you royalty?"

"Keep it down," Coren said, throwing a look around even though their low voices couldn't possibly be overhead in the havoc that was the streets of Oolum. "Yes, yes, it sort of does."

"Does that mean you're destined for a throne?"

"What? No!" Panic filled both his tone and his head. It was true that with Errance gone there were no other heirs, beyond his parents, and then himself, but Rendar was a Celestial elf, wasn't he? Didn't that just about guarantee he'd live forever?

"I want to meet these fancy parents of yours," Zizain drawled.

"I'd really rather you didn't."

"Why, do they have prejudice against short people?"

He laughed at the pert tilt of her head, but inside, he sobered. Yes, he could just see trying to explain to his parents why he was running around with a young woman, very much unmarried. He could see the expression in their eyes as they imagined all their worst fears about him coming true. And maybe he could explain it. Maybe they would believe it. But maybe there would be doubt in their hearts. Really, he just wanted to protect Zizain from the awkwardness of such a meeting. Or maybe he was protecting himself. Either way, he couldn't see any benefit from trying. This was his world now and he wasn't sure it could ever mesh with the world he had left behind.

Their conversation had traveled with them through the streets, and now the smell of sizzling onion and potatoes slowed their steps, turned them back around, and brought them to a booth from where the pops and cracks of hot oil sounded. "Two wraps, if you please," Coren said, digging into the purse concealed in the sash around his waist.

"My treat today, Cap'n," Zizain said with a slap against his arm.

"Aye, with my coin."

"Your coin? I earned this without you, thank you very much." They accepted the wrapped flatbread bursting with onion, potato, and hummus, blowing on it to cool their burning fingers. "Found an old band I used to dance with, bounced right back in. Got all sorts of coin, though I had to split it with the boys. Unfair, I say, since they weren't making anything until I joined."

He wasn't sure how she managed the balance. There was no doubt that she loved to dance and she loved to perform. And yet, he could see when the smile upon her face turned into the gritting of teeth and the brightness of her eye became a glint. She loved the attention, and she hated it. Hated those who made the crude comments, the leers, the sneers. Would that he could give her a just world where she danced for the pleasure of it and all those watching merely appreciated her talent.

"You do know you don't have to dance for coin if that's what you're worried about. Business is regaining ground, so you don't have to stress on that account."

"Who said I was worried and stressed, eh?"

"I just don't want you pushing yourself into anything you're uncomfortable—"

"You don't want?" She took a few dancing steps in front of him and stopped, forcing him to pull up short. Standing on her tiptoes, she gave him an appraising look. "Why are you worried about me dancing again? You jealous?" Her rich brown eyes sparkled inches from his. This close, he could see the bits of gold floating in their depths, like mica in the soil of a forest stream.

Why! Why must she keep testing him? Alright, fine, he knew why. But he wished she would stop. He couldn't deny that it hurt him in some way. The teasing sent a longing through his heart, a curiosity of what it would be like to love her. But he had to stop it fast each time. Because she didn't mean it. She really didn't. For all her mockery, he could see the pain that flashed through her eyes, her distrust, her unshakeable belief in betrayal. She didn't trust romance in the slightest. But if he could at least help her trust love in friendship, then that would be enough.

After a few moments, she pulled back from his face, the grin on her mouth broadening.

He exhaled. "Jealousy has nothing to do with my reasons for not wanting vile men to eye you up and down." All right, so maybe there was a tad bit of jealousy, but he liked to think it was a healthy kind.

He wasn't sure when it had started. Her behavior certainly never changed. Teasing him seemed to be her secret delight, although perhaps she was more delighted than ever since discovering his race. But his response...he didn't know...it had used to be just exasperation. Slowly, over time, this other longing had snuck in. There was something about her—even though he'd had many close friends over the years, there was this warmth between them he treasured, a trust and joy like he hadn't experienced with anyone else.

Oh well. What they had was special; there was no doubt about that. He wasn't going to ruin it by trying to make it into something else.

13

OOLUM

Past

"Excuse me?" The voice was soft, whisper-thin really, but somehow he heard it above the bustle of voices as people ate their meals and soothed their fretful children. He turned and found a young woman he recognized.

Her name was Maia, and she'd been coming to the meals for some time now, even before the roundness of her belly had become obvious. Zizain had offered to help with the birth several times as the days for delivery approached, but she'd always shaken her head with those wide eyes as timid and dark as a doe's. Now the baby lay cradled against her chest, but the fear had never left the young mother's face.

Coren knew why. He'd seen the mark on the inside of her wrist several times. One of the girls belonging to the Ichibol Harem, one of Oolum's largest brothels.

"What can I help you with, Maia?" he asked with a friendly smile, trying not to let any surprise show. She never spoke to him if she could help it, going instead to Zizain with any of her questions or requests.

"I need to speak to you and Zizain," she murmured. "In private." The sleeping baby in her arms squirmed and she tightened her grip, the lines on her face becoming more pronounced.

"Sure, Maia, sure." He kept his tone light, casual, soft enough not to be overheard. "We can step into the storeroom." He looked across the square for Zizain and found her already staring at them in curiosity. A small flick of his head brought her over.

"Fever, is it?" Zizain said, not missing a beat. She wrapped an arm around Maia's shoulders and guided her through the entry into the dusky storeroom, letting the door creak shut behind the three of them.

"It's not a fever," Maia said, brow wrinkling in confusion.

"I know that, darling, but any listening ears need an explanation. What is it really about?"

Maia took a look at the door as if it wasn't thick enough, her expression somehow becoming even more distressed. With the mention of listening ears, her voice dropped yet lower so that Coren had to lean forward a bit to hear.

"I want you…to take…Telinah."

"Who is—" Coren began, but then knew it was a stupid question. He stared down at the tiny baby in her arms, his heart sinking.

"I don't want her to…live the life I've lived," Maia continued. "I want her with you. Safe. If you can't keep her, find someone else. I will tell them something. I will find some explanation. It is not uncommon for our babies to die."

Did Ichibol Harem even need to "recruit" any workers if they allowed their women to give birth? But as she implied, the number of children who survived their chances of being born diseased or considered too homely was probably thin. And those who did live would know nothing but a life of slavery, girl or boy. Both fates made him sick.

"Maia," Coren said gently. "It seems to me that someone who loves her child so very much should not be separated."

Distress flared in the girl's eyes. "She must! She cannot stay with me! Please, you must take her!"

"We will," Coren promised, watching the relief flood into her face. And then he said, "But you can come with her."

Zizain made a small choking sound, but it was drowned out by the shrill intake of breath as Maia retreated a step. "No," the young mother gasped, "No, I cannot. They will find me."

"I have ships departing to Dormandy all the time," Coren said, taking a seat upon a crate. "And I have friends in West Orim, particularly a former crewmate who now lives in a small town north of Dormandy. We used to rescue slaves from the islands, and he and his family are very good people. If we smuggle you across the ocean, you'll be in free territory and safe in a small, distant town. You said it is not uncommon for babies from the Harem to die, but I suppose it is not uncommon for their women and men to die or disappear either. You don't need to stay here, Maia. You can start over. We'll take you and Telinah to freedom. You have my word."

Her feet shuffled on the floor. "I don't know."

"I have a shipment scheduled to leave for Dormandy two days from now. Think it over and let me know the eve before departure. We'll sneak you aboard and no one but us and the most trusted of my crew members will know."

She looked a bit startled at that last bit, so he quickly added, "And my most trusted crew members will only know that we're smuggling someone, not who that someone is. Trust me, they're used to it."

"You've smuggled people before?" It was a startling enough revelation to make her lift her head and look at him.

"Aye. But only people in need of rescue. So you have nothing to fear. Captain Coren of the *Solitary Star* will see you safely across the sea."

Something like hope, or at least the beginnings of it, flickered in Maia's eyes and she bobbed a bow before turning to leave.

"Wait!" Zizain flung out a hand to halt her, then turned to a shelf of bottles and dug around till she found a small vial. "A tincture for the fever," she said with a helpful smile. "In case anybody asks."

Maia bobbed again to both of them, then scuttled away.

When the door had shut behind her and the sounds of her footsteps had faded, a small breath fluttered from Coren's spreading smile. "Finally."

Zizain leaned against the door, her arms crossed, her brows raised. "Finally?" she echoed.

He began to pace, hands running through his hair. He could barely speak past the excitement racing through his veins. "I've been praying for some opportunity to help the slaves here. Some beginning. And here it is. The first step."

"So, in other words," Zizain said slowly. "You don't plan on Maia being a one-time rescue, you intend to start smuggling more."

Even caught as he was in spinning visions of the future, he couldn't miss the tension in her tone. He paused, looking askance. "What's the matter, Zizain? We've spoken of it before. You can't stand the sensual slave trade any more than I can."

"Of course I can't stand it. And I'd love to rescue those kids. But you've got to be smart about this. You can't leave a trail."

"This isn't my first smuggling job, Zi."

"If you're planning to make a habit of it, you'll need to be even more careful," she snapped. "Maybe you can rescue a girl or two from some random cads, but if you plan on starting to rob the brothels of their wares, people are going to start trying to catch you. You can't just start inviting all troubled women in this city to be spirited away on the wings of your red ship. There are plenty who would report you if it got them some extra coin. Oolum won't just give you a slap on the wrist. Their merchant council thrives off of this trade. They would have you killed."

"So we'll be careful!" Coren said, flashing a sun-bright grin. "In fact...we won't even be us. Haven't you always wanted to be a tall, rich woman?"

Her nose wrinkled up in several folds. "Eh? No."

"But you could be." He circled her, fingers tapping his chin. "Some especially tall heels, some added weight, heavy kohl eyes, new hairstyle, new clothes. I could make you look like a different person altogether. A Madame perhaps. We could always buy the freedom of a few with guises like that."

"And while I'm a tall, rich woman, what will you be?" she demanded, hands on outraged hips.

"Whatever I want, I suppose! If I could convince everyone I'm human, then I'm sure I could branch out to different types of human."

"You could try being shorter," Zizain said crossly before she flounced away.

Maia did not appear at any of the meals the entire next day. On the morning of the second day, as they passed out a breakfast of flat cakes, a gnawing fear began to chew at the back of Coren's mind.

"Why isn't she here?" he muttered. "I told her to give us her decision this evening, but I wasn't expecting her to ghost us before that."

"Maybe the idea scared her away," Zizain said with a shrug. "It's not an easy decision to make."

"Maybe..." He caught sight of a familiar woman from the tail of his vision and veered to intercept her before she could take a cake from one of the other helpers and disappear. It was one of the other women from the Ichibol Harem, who never stayed long or wanted to be noticed. "Iye," he called, motioning her away from the crowd. "Have you seen Maia? Do you know why she is not here this morning?"

Looking slightly discomfited to be asked about an associate, Iye shifted from foot to foot, looking anywhere but at him. "She was bought yesterday," she muttered. "Her and her baby. By Lord Ehbei."

It was all Coren could do not to curse out loud. He knew the name vaguely, but the name didn't matter as much as the circumstance. The brothels did not usually sell off their workers, unless for an exceptional price. For some girls it would be a dream to be bought by a rich lord, hoping for better housing and food. But Coren doubted it was Maia's dream, especially not when she'd wanted her daughter to know freedom.

"Thank you, Iye," he said only, handing her an extra flat cake, which she took before darting away.

"What was that about?" Zizain asked, trotting up alongside him.

"Lord Ehbei bought Maia and Telinah."

"Eiiii," she trilled softly, shaking her head. "That's that, then. He's known for his collection of pretty women. He would definitely notice if one of them went missing."

"I'm not giving up just like that!" he exclaimed. "Come on." He stalked down the street till he reached their safe house, Zizain following, and closed the door behind them. He threw open the hatch to their cellar and only when they were tucked into the dark, a single candle lit between them, did he continue speaking. "We can still figure out a way to get to her on that ship. And before you say it's too dangerous, I'm aware Ehbei would be more likely to try and track the thieves down, but we wouldn't be caught. Not if there is someone else he would be more than happy to blame."

"You mean we set it up to look like the work of a rival." A spark of mischief replaced the worry in Zizain's eyes, and she leaned back, tapping her chin. "These rich lords always have rivals."

"Exactly. We just have to do a bit of digging. Find out which of his competitors is most likely to pull such a stunt and how we can leave clues to that direction."

"More importantly, find out how we sneak in and out of a lord's estate with one of his women and a baby," she said, a dour scowl returning to her mouth.

Coren winked. "Don't worry, that's the fun part."

14

It was at the tail end of mid-day that they returned to the safe house, a trailing shadow of snooping and shenanigans stretching out behind them. Each had gone their own path to their own sources with their own knack of gossiping about nothing and hearing about everything.

Zizain had a whole package of baklava now in her possession, which she greedily did not offer to share. "So, so, what did you find out?" She popped a bit of the baklava into her mouth, chewing loudly.

"He has a rival, sure enough," Coren said, cracking his knuckles as he took a seat on the nearest crate. A wicked little smile curled his lip. "A half-brother."

"Ohhh, the half-brother rivalries are the worst," she said, with a knowing sort of nod, even though she, in fact, did not have siblings of any kind, at least any known about.

"As fate would have it, they are often competitors when it comes to buying fine slaves at auctions or fine anything really. Both rich, both corrupt, both hate each other's guts. It couldn't be set up more perfectly. Whoever we go in as, we leave tracks that lead straight back to his brother, Lord Yhaeb. He won't question it because he won't want to. Any excuse for him to take his brother to court or pay back revenge in another way is a good excuse."

"And I think I have our cover," she said, swallowing her last bit of food with a satisfying smack. "After some poking around, I heard who goes in and out of his estate. It seems he is often visited by a fortune teller. She goes by the name of Seer Ahlih. Lives in a richer part of the city, but not so much that we couldn't visit. Not so rich that she couldn't be bought off."

"Good. Let's get dressed up and pay her a visit then." He slapped his knees and made to stand, but Zizain caught his arm with her sticky fingers.

That former worry in her eyes gleamed amber in the weak candlelight. "We shouldn't rush it. Maia doesn't have to take the ship tomorrow. We could always take another ship."

Coren shook his head. "The weather suggests it will be a fast passage across the strait, and once we rescue her, we would need to get her out of the city at once. We can't just leave her there, resigned to her fate. Don't fear, I'm not going to get clumsy just because I'm moving fast."

After a moment, Zizain's grip loosened and she nodded.

As Zizain had said, Seer Ahlih was not so impossible to reach. If you wore the right clothes and walked the sort of walk that said you belonged on this street, nobody questioned you at all.

In this part of the city, most of the houses were finely built, holding a shop on the lower floor and the living quarters on the second floor. Most didn't have signs, just enough decoration outside their doors for you to more or less guess what was inside. For example, that one building that had layers of brightly colored cloth hanging from its windows, doors, and overhangs and smelled of pungent mordant no doubt belonged to a dye shop. And the one they stood in front of now— hung with chimes, strings of herbs, its red door painted over with glyphs and eyes to ward off evil spirits—most certainly belonged to a fortune teller.

Coren rapped on the door and when a mousy servant boy opened it with a bit of suspicion, he pressed a coin into the lad's hand. "Seer Ahlih expects us," he said only.

The boy nodded and led them in past a waiting room filled with pillows and braziers of incense and into a smaller shadowed room surrounded by strings of beads and shells. A portly woman dressed in fine purple fabric (probably traded from her neighbor next door) sat on the center pillow, but her posture indicated she'd dozed off rather than meditated.

She startled when the beads jangled to announce their entrance. Her kohl-rimmed eyes blinked hard to get a look at them. "Who is that, boy? Haven't I told you not to disturb me at these times? No customer was to come in now."

"But he said..." the boy began.

"I assured him you were expecting us," Coren said smoothly. "With a skill like yours, how could you not foresee the day that the winds would change for you? A change for the better at that."

Her glare sharpened, but it gained an edge of curiosity. He wore rich, brightly colored garb of fine fabric and design that might have belonged to either a merchant or a lord, but certainly someone seeking to stand out. He'd dusted his skin to a deep bronze and trimmed his jaw and lip with a black beard. Zizain wore heavy white linen covering her from veiled head to slippered toe, vague and mysterious enough to leave one wondering if she was a temple priestess or some secretive house servant.

Recovering, the woman straightened. "Of course I know when the winds change," she said, lifting her chin. At a flick of a hand, the boy scurried away, and with another flick, she motioned them to sit down.

"You go to see Lord Ehbei tonight, yes?" Coren said, but there was no doubt in his question.

"What business is it of yours?" she snapped.

"Consider it the business of Lord Yhaeb," he answered and watched for the moment that she recognized the name and the connection. It didn't take long; apparently the brothers' rivalry was at a forefront of Ehbei's life. "It is my lord's request," he went on, "that you do not go and visit Lord Ehbei tonight, but that you send another fortune teller in your stead. The humble servants you see before you now." He reached into the thick sash folded about his waist and withdrew a pouch of coins that he tossed to the floor at her feet. "It is just a little favor."

The seer pulled the pouch towards her and poked through it, biting one coin. "You think I will lose my position with Lord Ehbei just to win the favor of a lord no different and no richer? I cannot think of anything Lord Yhaeb could offer me that I'm not receiving already."

"You need not lose your position. You can have the favor of both. All you have to do is send us in your stead tonight. We shall give him a pleasing, if a bit misguided future, which will promise him seeking your services more than ever. It benefits all of us."

"I suppose that could be profitable." She turned the coin over in her fingers.

"It could be though," Coren said with a sage nod. "It could be."

The seer lent them her wagon, a colorful painted box pulled by a single white donkey. It was only big enough for one person so Zizain sat inside, curtains drawn, and Coren led the donkey by the bridle.

The rich of the city lived apart from the rest in a walled and gated quarter. Coren handed the Seer's card to the gatekeepers and they passed through with no difficulty. Light was beginning to fade from the sky by the time they reached Lord Ehbei's estate.

Sharp citrus aromas drifted from his courtyard, the leaves of orange trees peeking over the walls. Coren tethered the donkey to the trough beside the road, patting its neck as it took long slurps of water, and then went to the carriage box, helping Zizain out with a lift of his hand.

The two of them approached the guards standing at the lord's courtyard door, but the sight of the seer's wagon was familiar enough for the men to bow and stand aside, ushering them through. A secondary guard at the main doors walked them inside and announced the arrival of Seer Ahlih with a voice that boomed through the large domed room.

Not a moment later, a man appeared at the top of the marble stair, his waxed beard glistening even at a distance. Folding his ringed hands on his stomach, he came hurrying down towards them, but stopped still a few steps away from the floor. His eyes narrowed. "You are not Seer Ahlih!" he exclaimed. "How dare you enter my presence without my blessing!"

Their escort startled at the accusation, his hand darting to the scimitar at his side.

Before anyone could make so much as a move towards them, Coren bowed low enough that his head almost touched his knees. "Forgive us, forgive us, my lord, we are not Seer Ahlih, but we come in her stead and with her blessing."

Lord Ehbei considered that for a few moments and his guard remained frozen, waiting for a signal. "She has never sent any other in her stead," the lord said at last with a frown. "Is she ill?"

"She received a vision that left her faint. So we have come to see the future for you, oh Lord Ehbei, may you live past the stars."

A bit pacified, the lord took the final few steps down the stair and approached them, eying Zizain. "Is she any good?" he asked, peering at the heavy veil as if he could see something through it.

"Ah, Lord Ehbei, she is not the seer," Coren said, waving his hand to dismiss the idea from existence. His moustache titled upwards with his smile. "I am."

"You?" He drew back, raising an arm in distaste as if it could be a wall between them. "I only have taken the services of women fortune tellers."

Coren swayed forward in response. "Look into my eyes, my lord, are they not very green?"

The lord hesitated, brow wrinkling. "They are...they are very green."

"They are green because of the fertile futures they see, my lord. These green eyes will find great things in your life, trust this one."

"I suppose...I suppose I could try you this once. But I want Seer Ahlih back as soon as she recovers."

"Of course, of course. Let me send my servant out to the gardens to burn incense and offer prayers on your behalf."

"Yes, yes, have her do that," Ehbei said, waving Zizain from the room with a flick of his hand and gesturing towards a curtained room. "Come and sit. The room is prepared as Seer Ahlih prefers it; let me know if you require anything different."

Coren kept his eyes fixed ahead, refusing to follow the movement of Zizain's veiled figure as she floated across the floor towards the garden entrance. Instead, he followed the lord past a drawn back curtain into a dark, windowless room. The walls were covered in tapestry and the floors lined with thick, lush pillows. Little censers of incense hung from the ceiling or sat on low tables, along with clusters of dried herbs and crystals. This man clearly hung a lot on knowing his future if he had an entire room dedicated to the seer's preference.

Thanking God that his nose had long since adjusted to pungent smells, Coren sat amid the pillows and drew out a silk wrapped orb from the tasque bound to his waist. He shook off the cloth and set the glass ball down upon a dimpled pillow. The seer may have parted with her carriage for a sum of money, but she certainly had not parted with any tools of her trade, so the glass ball Coren had found was really nothing more than something that might have decorated a garden or a courtyard wall.

"Sit, my friend, sit." Coren waved a hand at the lord. He rubbed his hands against his silken trousers, trying to hide the damp sheen on his palms. To be perfectly honest, he had not really stopped to observe fortunetellers in the past, really only knew about them by reputation, so if he made a wreck of this, he could only hope the man would attribute it to 'personal style.'

"Close your eyes, let your mind empty, so I may gaze clearly into your future."

The man did so, giving him a moment to breathe and think.

About now, Zizain would have found a spot to hide in the gardens and be changing into the clothes of an older servant woman. Then she would head for the nursery attached to the harem. It might take some convincing to let her inside if they were not expecting a nursemaid, but she was better than anyone at making herself belong somewhere, that he knew well. Once inside, she would have to find Maia and get her and the baby away quietly so she could tell her the rest of the plan.

All right, enough stalling. Taking a deep breath, Coren hummed under his breath. "Place your hands upon my crystal ball," he said. Really, he should have done some study about this, but there had not been time.

Ehbei did so, looking a little mystified, but also intrigued, so that was better than suspicion.

"Ah, ah, yes," Coren said, squinting down into the glass. "Yes, you are a man of great influence, and lavish wealth. What was given to you has been increased by your own ambition. But there was another, was there not? Someone who sprouted up from the same fertile soil, who has clung to your gardens like a noxious weed."

Ehbei's mouth twisted in a subtle growl, his bearded chin dipping in acknowledgment.

"You and your brother have struggled for years, trying to outdo the other in power and wealth, and even now, he plots against you. He plots what he might steal, jealous of the size of your coffers and your harems."

"I knew it, I knew it," the man said, teeth grinding together.

"But as time goes on, oh mighty Ehbei, your trowel will cut out the weeds and your garden will flourish. What little ground he gains will be lost. Do not fear, oh lord, for your fortune is most secure."

"*Is* it? Tell me more about it."

Well, he did need to buy time, that was for certain. Nothing for it, he'd just come up with things on the fly. "The favor of one whose wealth is greater will fall upon you, and he shall give you the hand of his beautiful daughter. As the sun sets, so it must rise, and you will rise in this man's stead, but greater than he. The crops of your trees will bear much fruit. Your children will outnumber them by far, but they will honor their sire. No sickness will take hold of you, for the blessings of many gods will be upon you. Even the leaders of this city, yes, even the great guild will listen to your words."

"And?"

Something mixed between pity and disgust twisted Coren's heart. What sort of man really was so insecure and greedy with his life that he wanted to know every detail of what might happen? And since he sent for the seer so regularly, he surely received conflicting answers from time to time. Did he really believe any of it? Or was it just grasping for some self-satisfaction?

He cleared his throat. "And the glass goes dim, I see nothing more. The visions withdraw for now."

The man leaned back, a measure of calm returning to his eyes. "Very well then, very well. I must say, Seer, you pleased me well. Perhaps I will send for you another time."

"It is impossible, my lord, for this was my last visit in the city of Oolum. I head to Brivan on the morrow." He stood, gathering up his things and bowing low.

"Brivan?" Lord Ehbei scoffed. "What can Brivan offer you that Oolum can't?"

"The court of the Tharmane, oh gracious lord."

The man's jaw went slack at that and it took him a few attempts to recover. No matter how affluent he was, there was no way to compete with the favor of the Tharmane, the ruling absolute of mysterious and exotic Brivan, proclaimed a god by his priests.

"May his brightness smile upon you," he murmured at last, almost forgetting himself and dipping a small little bow of his own.

The veiled servant girl stood just outside when Coren and the lord stepped past the curtain, her hands demurely folded in front of her.

Coren bowed to the lord with final parting blessings, then led the way out of the grand house. He walked her to the waiting carriage and opened the door to let her inside, and only then did a small voice whisper from behind the veils, "Where is Zizain and my baby?"

"It is all right, Maia," Coren said quietly, helping her inside and moving to close the door. "We will be stopping on the next corner and waiting for her to catch up."

She nodded, her form hunched and frightened even underneath all the swathes of fabric. "I….I did not think you would come for me," she murmured. "I thought it was all over. I couldn't believe it when I heard Zizain's voice and I...I can barely recognize you even now."

"Clever, aren't we?" He clicked the door shut behind her, undid the donkey's tether, and headed down the road. His footsteps were calm and quiet in the sand, nothing like the loud beating of his heart.

It had worked, it had actually worked, but it wasn't over yet. Zizain still had to arrive, both her and the baby. Choosing to take the baby with her had been risky, as a child separated from its mother was likely to cry. But changing places beneath the veils was the only idea they'd had, and if the baby had cried or moved while in front of the lord, then it would have been all over. With Zizain at least, she would have the excuse of being a midwife taking the child somewhere for care.

There.

There she was, just as promised, standing at the corner with a laundry basket. She did not look at them but began ambling the same direction, just slow enough that Coren and the carriage were able to pull up alongside her.

"Looks like a heavy load," he said casually, coming to a stop and opening the door to the carriage. "How about you set it inside?"

"That would certainly take the weight off my poor back," Zizain said with a snort, reaching in to set it gently on the carriage floor. Maia lifted off the top blanket in the basket, exhaling in a soft murmur at the sight of her baby sleeping on the blankets folded underneath, and gathered her up into her arms. Coren closed the door again, sharing a victorious smile with his partner.

There was still a ways to go yet. Zizain would take a different path to their rendezvous and then take Maia and her baby from the carriage to a safe house. Coren would return the borrowed carriage to the Seer. And from there, they would simply have to wait the night until they could sail on the following day.

But just now, seeing that look of relief on Maia's face as she was reunited with her daughter, it felt like they had already won.

15

I t was a perfect morning to sail on the seas. The temperatures had dropped low in the night, allowing the new day to start crisp and refreshed. Thin, wispy clouds feathered the sky high above, suggesting that wind would be in their sails without threatening an oncoming storm. Coren had overseen the packing of his crates in the warehouse the night before and now he stood at the docks as a freight inspector poked through his cargo.

This particular inspector he'd never seen without a scowl, no matter how Coren would smile or joke. He always examined the cargo with the look of one expecting to find something incriminating, as if that would be the only thing that would perk his mood. It just had to be him. Not any of the inspectors whom Coren could share a good laugh and story with, no, it had to be this one.

On all days, when Coren did have something incriminating in his cargo.

Coren had prepared a crate just for Maia and Telinah. The lower third of the crate was a compartment for her to lie down in. When the hatch was closed above her, heavy fabrics were set on top. The floor of her compartment was lined with a thick blanket, both to cushion her as much as possible, and to block out light between the crate slats. There were of course the slats and holes left open to allow her and her baby to breathe. It would hardly be comfortable, as closely confined as it was, but it was the best he could do until she was on his ship and he could move her to the smuggling room Ulio had built into the hull. The baby would be quiet for a while, lulled to deep sleep with a gentle blend of herb tincture.

"Beautiful day, isn't it, Inspector!" Zizain said cheerfully, appearing alongside Coren's elbow.

The inspector actually raised his head with an expression other than a scowl. It wasn't anywhere close to a smile, but perhaps mild curiosity. "And what are you doing here, Zizain?" he inquired.

Coren shouldn't have been surprised by now that almost everybody seemed to know Zizain, but he still had to swallow a cough.

"Today, I'm a sailor," she declared, stiffening her posture in what was the most dramatic and mocking stand of attention that he'd ever seen. "This redheaded rascal is finally taking me out to see the sea, see?"

The man nodded, never mind the last few words had sounded like a string of unending "z's." He turned a slight frown Coren's way. "You watch those sailors of yours, you hear?"

"Sir, you'll not find better behaved or better natured men on these seas than my sailors," Coren said pleasantly. "But thank you, all the same. I'm glad to find another friend of Zizain's."

He couldn't deny it unsettled him a little bit to bring Zizain on a voyage for the first time. It wasn't as if he expected any trouble, he just wasn't so sure how he felt about breaking one of his rules. But he needed her with Maia and the little one, needed her to be sure they would be taken care of while he guided the ship. And anyway. Zizain was truly a part of the crew by now even if she hadn't taken a passage with them yet. As for the crew, none of them seemed to mind; instead they were amused and delighted by her company.

And with that, the inspector waved them on their way.

It had been a while since the *Solitary Star* had moved with such speed across the waters, it was as if she knew that her mission was precious. Coren hardly had to steer her straight, the currents led so true. At this rate, they'd reach Dormandy's harbor before the sun set and settle for the night at an inn.

But just as he was sending up a quick prayer of thanks, he noticed Zizain appear from the hold of the ship and hurry towards him.

"It's the baby, Coren," Zizain said in a low voice when she reached him. "We gave her some milk, but it's not enough to keep her from wailing. She can be overheard if it's quiet enough."

Coren's hands twitched on the wheel. Really, with the creaking of the wood and the deep hum of the ocean, not to mention a deck and galley full of sailors, nobody, absolutely nobody should notice the crying of one small baby. And even if they did hear it, his men would know better than to ask questions or complain. But there was still that risk of just enough stir to loosen tongues. A simple thing where sailors might speak of that time a baby screamed the whole way across the strait, and if the wrong ears overheard, questions might be asked.

He stared at Zizain a moment longer and watched as the intense gleam in her eye sharpened with some sudden, wicked little thought. A smile curved her lips and she spun away from him, prancing down the stairs.

"Are all trips this dull?" she hollered. "Aren't sailors supposed to be singing their shanties all night long? How about some music, mates?"

As if one body, the sailors perked and started to move, but then paused and flung an askance glance Coren's way.

"You heard her, lads," Coren called. "Give her a song."

Boots and bare feet thundered on the ground in a mad scrabble as men raced for their instruments, some hidden somewhere close at hand, some kept down below by their hammocks. An assortment of the fellows finally gathered, arguing over tunes, and fiddling with their instruments. It took a few more minutes before a song finally limped into motion, then strengthened into a lively jig. Fife, accordion, mandolin, drum…they each knew their part, even if it took them a while to agree. The song twirled, the musician's feet tapped.

But instead of leaping into dance, Zizain remained frozen on the wooden floor, her hand fiddling against the crook of the other arm. It was such an abashed pose that Coren was taken aback. It couldn't be that she was shy now, could it? Would she rather dance for strangers than for his own crew? Well. Now that he put it that way, he could see where the embarrassment might be coming from.

Her face lifted and her gaze snapped across the deck to where he stood at the prow. The shyness was gone so fast he could have almost believed he'd made it up. Her bare foot stamped on the wooden deck at the same time that her finger stabbed towards him and then downwards. The sailors looked to where she pointed and laughed, heads tilted in curiosity for his response.

"Come on, Cap'n!" one of the men hollered. "The first mate says he's seen you throw a jig or two."

"Aye, don't be shy," another shouted.

As if by magic his first mate was suddenly at his side, politely ready to take the wheel.

Coren shot him a look. "Seen me throw a jig or two? I've thrown a jig or three, thank you very much."

"I wasn't counting," the man replied. "But I'll start now, if you like."

Coren hopped down the steps, taking off his boots and tossing them to the side as he went. He didn't fancy himself a clumsy dancer, but he didn't wish to chance stepping on Zizain's toes, and anyway, he liked the feel of the sun-weathered wood beneath his bare soles.

He reached out his hand, and her fingers wrapped around his, whisking him forward. A bright orange ribbon of music caught underneath them, spinning them together, apart, and back again. Flashes of blue sky, red sail, and Zizain's white smile danced across Coren's vision, a kaleidoscope of joyful color. Bursts of laughter caught between their gasps for breath as they danced madly across the planks, the music ever rising. At some point, some of the sailors joined in, and Zizain spun away from him to dart from partner to partner, only to whirl back to his hand once more.

And so the music carried them across the sea and to the land beyond.

16

The day that Maia had approached them, Coren sent a letter oversea to his former mate so that it would arrive a few days before them. He knew the man and his family would be flexible enough to help anyone in need, even if they appeared suddenly at their doorstep, but a little preparation would be better for everyone involved.

On the morning after the voyage, he rented a wagon just outside the city of Dormandy, while Zizain and the fugitive mother waited at a distance. Zizain sat with him on the front seat, Maia nested in a bundle of blankets in the wagon bed. He'd chosen a wagon with the bows to put up the canvas in case of rain or unfriendly eyes, but the sky was not clouded and the road was not crowded, so their day-long travel to the outskirt town of Lire was uneventful.

Zizain couldn't seem to go fifteen minutes without making some comment on the landscape. "I always heard the grass was greener on the other side of the sea," she remarked, "But I never expected there'd be this much of it. Brights, it just stretches on forever, doesn't it?"

"There are a lot more valleys in it then you would expect, same as the sand dunes," Coren said. "And once summer hits, the grass will dry up to a plain yellow-brown. But I suppose it is beautiful even so." He squinted at the dark hedge along a distant dell. "I'm partial to the forests myself."

"I tried venturing out to the jungle when I was younger once," Zizain informed. "Nasty thing, that. Felt like it wanted to boil me in my own sweat and leave my body to the bugs."

"The forests aren't like that here," Coren said softly. "They're cool. Quiet. Mysterious. Grand, even."

Zizain opened her mouth, perhaps to ask more about the forests he once had known, but threw a glance back at the sleeping Maia and thought better of it. In a way, Coren was sorry. He would have liked to tell her more.

"Do they smell like you?" she asked suddenly.

Coren snorted in surprise. "Pardon?"

"There's always this crisp, sharp smell lingering about you, so long as there isn't a stench nearby overpowering it. I always used to assume it was some sort of incense you liked to wear, but," she threw one more glance at Maia and leaned forward to whisper, "but I once heard it said that your kind smells like the trees."

"The evergreens," Coren said wistfully, imagining the silver green boughs swaying in the wind. "I suppose I hadn't noticed, just assumed it wore off, I guess."

"It has not," she said with a significant nod. Suddenly she stood up in the seat, her hand against his shoulder for balance. "There! Is that the town?"

"So it is." He clucked to the oxen and flicked the reins to hurry their plodding steps, but they'd caught sight of the town already and quickened their pace in the hope of stables and hay, perhaps even grain.

Maia shifted, straightening and crawling to the front. "Are we here?" she rasped, voice scratchy from little use. She clutched at the wrap holding her baby about her chest. "You are sure…you are sure they know we are coming?"

"Aye." And even if the letter had been lost, it would be all right, although Coren did not want to say that and throw more doubt into her anxious mind.

"You are sure I will be welcome?"

"Aye."

"You are sure…" she faded off, leaving dozens of possibilities left unsaid. Sure that she would not be found out. Sure that this was the right choice. Sure that her baby could grow up healthy and happy. Perhaps she realized all the questions she could ask, and all the ways they could not be answered. And yet this was still her best way forward.

"Harson Thatch was one of my best mates some years back before he decided to settle down and start a family," Coren said anyway, repeating what he had told her several times already. It didn't hurt to remind her that he hadn't changed his story. "He runs the smithy in town and his wife, Nelsa Thatch is an accomplished seamstress. They have two children. The Thatchs have told me before they'd like to help people start over if they can, teaching either of their trades to anyone interested."

A few townsfolk looked at them as they rolled down the main street, but lost interest when they took a turn to a building on the outskirts. A small two-story house stood next to a blacksmith shop and stable. They had hardly pulled up the oxen when the door opened and a man and woman stepped out, two small children tagging at their heels.

"Not a day late, Coren!" the man called cheerfully. "Still ship-shape as ever, I see!"

"Maia, isn't it?" Missus Thatch said cheerfully, wiping her hands off on her apron and dipping into a curtsy.

Too overwhelmed to do anything but bob a timid nod, Maia held her child a bit closer to her chest, but that only brought Missus Thatch's attention to the baby.

"That must be your little Telinah? How about you follow me and we can get you both washed up and something to eat, hmm? I have a room upstairs prepared, it's all your own."

Maia threw Coren and Zizain an anxious look and he nodded for her to go ahead. "We'll be around, Maia. We'll stay for a few days and you can decide if you want to live here or not. And if you do decide to stay, we will write letters checking in on you often."

As the women headed in, Coren turned back to the oxen and with his old friend's help, pulled them to the stable to settle in for the night.

Only two days later, Coren and Zizain sat in the wagon again, noses pointed to Dormandy, the warmth of the sun on their backs almost as comforting as the way Maia had lit up in so short a time.

"It could have taken much longer for her to decide she wanted to stay," Zizain said aloud. "If we do things like this in the future, you should probably just let me stay with them till they adjust so you can get back to work."

"Back to work without you? How would I manage that?" Coren exclaimed.

"You seemed to manage before I came along, no?"

"Frankly, I'm not sure how."

She smiled a bit, settling in more comfortably beside him.

As they reached the fork in the road, he pulled back on the reins with a steady hand, drawing the oxen to a halt. One way would lead back to Dormandy. The other....well, the other pointed northwest, and he could see them from here—the beautiful blue mountains of Aselvia.

Aselvia.

An ache stabbed through his heart, sending his hand to clench a fist against his chest. How long had it been? He certainly hadn't been back since starting life in Oolum, and that had already been, oh, five years. And his visits before then had been sparse, in between his sea adventures with Ulio and his own brief explorations into other parts of Orim. Each time, his family had been overjoyed to have him back, and he couldn't deny that returning brought its own special joy. Joy that hadn't been without pain, because he hardly spoke of what he did beyond their borders. He told Oriah a little, especially of those harder, darker days that had left a scar upon his soul. He'd told Rendar other things, especially of the short foray up North where he hoped to have caught some word of Uncle Cerand (but the cold had quickly driven him back south.) But he had never told his parents much about his travels. It didn't seem to him they'd understand. In any case, they'd certainly find it too dangerous.

Still, he missed them.

Even if they didn't understand him, they…well, they cared, and after being out in this vast world a spell, he knew that was far more than could be said of some parents. They were gentle, good folk. They missed him, certainly.

But perhaps it was best he kept his wildness away. Maybe it would frighten them less.

He glanced down to find Zizain studying his expression, her head tilted slightly to the side, shaggy bangs spilling over the band about her brow. She followed his gaze to the distant mountains and the rolling hills

of forest. She looked back, more quizzical than ever. Not as if she didn't understand, but as if she did, and wanted to know his question.

Someday.

Someday, he'd go back, and well, if she was still with him—and he prayed to God she would be—he'd bring her along.

"Come on, Zizain," he said with a smile, turning his nose back east.

Back where the sea and the sand stretched as far as the eye could see.

"Let's go home."

17

OOLUM

Present

An amber shaft of light cut across the table beneath their hands as the sun triumphantly crested whatever buildings had impeded it.

"It is dawn," Coren said, rather amazed. Some part of him was aware the darkness had been lifting, but it still surprised him they'd talked through the night. He stood, stretching his back and shaking a leg that stung with the prickles of lingering numbness. "You must be hungry. Give me a moment, I'll start a fire and make some potato cakes."

Leoren merely stared across the room in some fixed trance. He was still in the same state after Coren had gone down to the larder and back up again.

"Hey," Coren said, nudging his shoulder gently with his elbow. "You fall asleep on me? Do you sleep with your eyes open?"

Leoren shifted, passing a hand over his face, eyelids fluttering. "Just thinking," he murmured. "I really have not…been the best father to you."

"It wasn't from lack of caring or trying," Coren said kindly. "I didn't exactly make it easy for you either."

"I could have tried more. I could have asked sooner for your perspective. Could have tried harder to understand."

"Well." He ruffled the hair at the back of his head. Honestly, he'd never thought there'd be a day when he spoke so fully from his heart to his father and be heard—actually heard. But then again, he'd never imagined the things that had happened in this past year. His father wasn't the only one to gain a new perspective—he'd been seeing sides of his daava he had never known existed, and well, he'd been colored a bit impressed. "I'm glad we are talking now. I'm glad you came. We've waited too long, I suppose, but better now than never."

"To everything its own time," Leoren said softly. "Ayeshune is good."

"He is certainly that."

"Morning, redhead!" Zizain's call came from outside the door a moment before she burst through it, one hand on the latch, one arm cradling the bundle wrapped to her chest. If she was abashed at all to see that there was a guest in the house, she showed no indication, but rather bounced to Coren's side and kissed him full on the cheek, turning her body so as not to squish the baby.

She turned to look at Leoren as he rose and if she had not been surprised there was a guest, she was certainly surprised as to his identity. "Lord Leoren!" she exclaimed.

"Please," Leoren said. "Please, just call me Leoren. Or Daava, if you want."

"Daava," Zizain echoed, a grin curling her lips. "That does have a nice ring to it, doesn't it? But what about grandpa in the elvish tongue?" She loosened the wrap about her body and pulled the chubby baby from its folds.

"Oh," Leoren said softly, taking the baby in his arms when she offered him. "Oh, he's grown so much already." He ran a finger through the wild tufts of his red hair and down to the smooth copper of his cheek. "Hello, Zoren. Do you remember your Ah'daava?"

The baby gave him a sour expression, no doubt offended to have left his mother's comforting embrace, but when his eyes focused on Leoren, a sliver of curiosity stole onto his face. He reached out and caught one of the strands of blonde hair dangling near his fist and gave it an experimental tug.

"Don't be pulling out Ah'daava's hair, he does enough of that over paperwork," Coren said, catching the tiny fingers and prying them open. "Brights, he's strong. I never understand how these little ones have such a grip."

"You were much the same," Leoren said, flicking his hair behind his back with expert ease.

"I'll get that breakfast going," Coren said, turning to the little clay oven. Where had that piece of flint gone? Glancing back to ask Zizain, he stopped, held fast by the sight before him.

The bright sunlight swept through the door, wrapping the figures in its touch with a warm, honey glow. His father rocked his little son in his arms, Zizain standing beside them, bright laughter in her eyes.

Some years ago, he wouldn't have guessed he'd be seeing such a scene now. But that's how life went, funny thing that it was. You could never tell what sort of adventure waited on the other side.

EPILOGUE

Wind and wave blew to and fro, and they carried many things upon them. The creatures of water and air rode upon their currents, and the ships of men needed both to guide them. No one could tell them where to go, only guess at what fate might have in store.

The same could be said of Captain Coren. For upon the sea or upon the sand, he wandered with little certainty of the road ahead. He only knew the calling upon his heart that surged like wind in the sails or the ocean roll beneath a prow. Many followed in his wake, caught in the thrill of a road untested. He carried the hopes and fears of countless souls upon him, striving to bring each to rest. Even his own hopes, which he carried lightly, found completion in a way better than he could have dreamed.

For who could say what guided stories but the same hand that brought in the tides and sent out the storms? And like the birds and ships upon the sea, his story would carry on, the wind and wave behind it.

ABOUT THE AUTHOR

From the beginning, H. S. J. Williams has loved stories and all the forms they take. Whether with word, art, or costume, she has always been fascinated with the magic of imagination. She lives in a real fantastical kingdom, the beautiful Pacific Northwest, with her very own array of animal friends and royally loving family. An artist as well as an author, she taught Fantasy Illustration at MSOA. She may also be a part-time elf.

SIGN UP FOR H.S.J. WILLIAMS'S NEWSLETTER FOR NEWS, ART, & SHORT STORIES!

www.hsjwilliams.com

BOOKS BY H.S.J. WILLIAMS

MOONSCRIPT

Book 1 of Kings of Aselvia

An elf prince imprisoned for seventy years. The unlikely children come to his rescue. A journey across foreign lands with their enemies in pursuit. The battle for his soul upon which the fate of a celestial kingdom hangs...

COLLUSION

Book 2 of Kings of Aselvia

An elf king struggles to overcome his past and embrace his future. When his beloved queen is stolen, he will set out into the world that once hurt him and comb through the dregs of the city to the heights of society. No web of deceit can stop him. .

FAIREST SON

A Gender-Swap Novella Retelling of Snow White

When a mortal huntress in pursuit of her prey comes across a scarred fae up in the cold mountains, she must choose her side in the battle between Seelie and Unseelie Courts. But she has secrets to hide that will ruin the new life she's been offered.

JOIN ELF

Educate. Liberate. Facilitate.

In this story and the rest of the series, the characters deal with bondage to great darkness and those bright few who seek to lead others to freedom.

That darkness is real in our own world, taking a similar form. The people who fight it are real too. Like Coren and Zizain, there are ministries reaching out to the needy on the streets or rescuing the hopeless from slavery.

But such ministries need awareness, prayer, and financial support. All Kindle purchases* of this book go towards these ministries! *Not including Kindle Unlimited or paperback.

Please consider looking into a ministry for the hurting that you can support, whether from this list or elsewhere.

Samaritan's Purse

Providing relief, resources, and redemption for disaster or poverty stricken areas.

Hagar International

Rescuing, healing, and empowering women and children survivors of slavery and abuse in violent regions such as Afghanistan, Cambodia, and Singapore.